Praise for Elmer Kelton

"Having written more than forty novels, Elmer Kelton has surely established himself as one of the grand masters of Western literature. A preeminent story-teller, Kelton has been blessed with the ability to create a cast of fictional characters which bring history to life with such honesty and believability that the reader himself literally becomes part of the story. . . . It is Kelton's understanding of human weaknesses and strengths that makes his writings so captivating. From this perspective, the reader is able to understand both sides of a conflict thus gaining a quiet empathy with the challenges each character must fact."
—*The El Paso Scene*

"Elmer Kelton is a Texas treasure, as important for his state as Willa Cather is for Nebraska and Badger Clark for South Dakota. Kelton truly deserves to be made one of the immortals of literature."
—*El Paso Herald-Post*

"Kelton's explanation of these men–cowboys without a future–is the strength of his writing. He understands them well, and his descriptiveness is simple, but complete. They are so familiar to him, so universal, their dialogue is seemless."
—*The Fort Worth Star-Telegram*

"You can never go wrong if you want to read a good story with realistic characters and you pick up a title by Elmer Kelton. . . . Kelton's characters jump off the page, they are so real."
—*American Cowboy*

"Elmer Kelton's Westerns are not filled with larger than life gunfighters who can shoot spurs off a cowboy's boots at 100 yards. They are filled with the kind of characters that no doubt made up the West. . . . They are ordinary people with ordinary problems, but Kelton makes us care about them."
—*Oklahoman*

Other Books by Elmer Kelton

Elmer Kelton

DARK THICKET

A TOM DOHERTY ASSOCIATES BOOK
NEW YORK

This is a work of fiction. All the characters and events portrayed in this book are either products of the author's imagination or are used fictitiously.

DARK THICKET

A Forge Book
Published by Tom Doherty Associates, LLC
175 Fith Avenue
New York, NY 10010

www.tor.com

Forge® is a registered trademark of Tom Doherty Associates, LLC.

ISBN 0-812-56522-3

Originally published in 1985 by Bantam Books.
First mass market edition: June 2001

Printed in the United States of America

0 9 8 7 6 5 4 3 2 1

along the way had Owen managed to beg oats o[r]
for him from some farmer he met, some strange[r]
[wh]ose barn he slept a night. The war had left littl[e]
[enou]gh even for people to eat, and horses must sustai[n]
[w]hatever grazing they could find. The fresh spring
[grass] was yet weak, and so was any animal that de-
[pend]ed upon it.

[O]wen came finally to a wagon trace which seemed to
[strik]e a chord in his memory. Turning in the saddle for
[a dif]ferent perspective, he thought he recalled using this
[trail] when he had traveled eastward two years and more
[ago] with his brother Ethan, eager to join the fighting
[befo]re it could all be finished without them. He found
[fami]liarity in the pitch of the gentle hills, the steeple of
[a di]stant church, the lay of a neglected cornfield with a
[gull]y started at its lower end, gradually carrying away
[the] fertile topsoil with every rain.

[A] mile ahead he saw a string of large wagons moving
[pon]derously toward him. They reminded him of the
[long] military supply trains he had seen early in the war,
[train]s that had gradually shortened as the Confederacy
[foun]d it difficult to keep filling them. These, he saw as
[they] came nearer, were heavy freight wagons paired in
[tand]em, each pair drawn by four spans of big draft
[hors]es and mules. He pulled out of the trail to yield them
[roo]m. A tired-looking middle-aged man on horseback
[rode] up to him. He gave Owen's bandaged arm a mo-
[ment']s study.

["H]owdy, soldier," he said pleasantly. "Where you
[heade]d?"

[Ow]en said, "Home. I'm Owen Danforth. You'd be
[Mr. T]isdale, wouldn't you?"

[Tis]dale blinked. "Owen?" His eyes narrowed for a
[closer], more careful look. "Damned if you ain't.

DARK
THICKET

Chapter 1

The war against the Union lay five wee[ks]
and he had crossed the Sabine out of
days ago. Owen Danforth was beginning
that he was truly back in Texas. Here, u
he was ready to return, the war would n

Until he was ready . . . A dull throbb
right hand up to grip his tightly bandag
all the fever had left it. He wondered
be ready to go back.

Late in the morning he had broker
and confining piney woods. Now h
higher, drier prairies that looked and
His rump itched with an urgency for
the afternoon sun was in his eyes, a
would catch him with miles yet to g
horse beneath him no longer took a l
The journey had been wearying, a

Wouldn't of knowed you, son. You've changed a right smart."

"So've you. When I left here you was farmin' on the river. You in the freightin' business now?"

Tisdale nodded. "War duty. I was too old to tote a rifle, and they said I'd do the government more service haulin' freight. I take cotton bales down to the Rio Grande and ferry them across to Mexico. Confederacy trades them to French and Englishmen for war supplies. The Yankees can bottle up the Texas ports, but they can't do nothin' about us tradin' in Mexico." He pointed his chin toward the lead wagon, its wide-rimmed wheels raising dust as they labored by. "I come north with guns and ammunition and such."

Owen had heard about the cotton trains. "I been told the Yankees invaded Brownsville from the sea to put a stop to this."

"They did. But we cross the Rio farther west, where their patrols can't reach. Then we travel down the river on the Mexican side and thumb our noses as we go by. Makes them madder'n hell." Tisdale looked at Owen's arm again. "If you're lookin' for work, I believe I can find somethin' you could do with one arm."

Owen shrugged. "Maybe later, after I see how things go with my folks. You seen them, Mr. Tisdale?"

Tisdale shook his head. "I been on the trail too much. It's all I can do to spend a night with the wife and young'uns when I pass through." He frowned. "I hear things, though. Seems like your old daddy's still got notions against the war. There's some fire-eatin' patriots that'd do him bodily harm if somebody was to just lead the way."

Owen grimaced, suddenly not sure he was in a hurry

to be home. "I ought to've known he wouldn't see reason."

Tisdale seemed hesitant to speak. "I *heard* you and him had a considerable disagreement when you left for the army."

"I was of age to make up my mind. So was my brother."

"Maybe the Lord's sent you at a good time. You bein' a wounded soldier come home, maybe the hotheads'll stand back and leave him alone. But you watch out, son. Things are touchy. There's been men killed for sayin' less than your daddy has."

Tisdale shook Owen's hand and fell into the dusty wake of the last wagon. Owen watched the train move away in its own slow time, and a sourness settled into his stomach.

Hell of a situation to come home to.

Gauging the position of the sun, he decided he should reach Uncle Zachariah Danforth's farm before dark. The tall bay horse needed rest, and Owen could better face the confrontation with his father if he arrived home fresh. Uncle Zach had been of the same mind as Andrew Danforth on the confederacy question and the war, but at least he could be tolerant of an opposing viewpoint. Tolerance was a seldom thing with Owen's father.

The left arm felt hot beneath the bandages, which had needed changing for the last two days. Now and then a sharp pain grabbed him with the violence of a cotton hook. Odd, he could not remember feeling any pain when the Yankee saber had slashed him. He had been caught up in the shouting fury of hand-to-hand fighting. Something about the fever of battle masked the pain until the excitement had peaked. Only then had he realized his arm was hanging uselessly, blood spilling from his sleeve and running down a dead-numb hand that could not feel its warmth. The first doctor who examined him was ready to saw the bone in two. Owen had fought like a cornered badger until the doctor turned away in his frustration, telling him to go ahead and die if that be his choice. Blood poisoning had nearly killed Owen, but he still had his arm. He could not yet tell whether it would ever be of use again.

He felt no rancor toward the doctor or even toward the faceless Yankee who struck him and rode on. He had no idea, for the excitement had been intense, whether the Yankee had been small or large, young or old. He did not know if the man had survived the fight. Many on both sides had not.

I'll be home tomorrow, he told himself. His mother would know what to do, what would be needed to draw out the fever and the poison. If the arm was to be saved, his mother would know how.

When the fever had been at its worst, the lifeline to which Owen had clung most tightly was an obligation to set things right with Andrew Danforth, to reconcile for careless and angry recriminations flung at their parting. Perhaps tomorrow he would find better words.

The sun was twenty minutes gone behind the great oak trees on the river when a turn of the trail and a clearing of the scattered timber showed him Zach Danforth's cabin in the dusk. Before he thought better, he touched spurs to the big horse and tried to bully a faster trot from him. He slowed, knowing he had taxed the animal too much already.

Uncle Zach had been a widower longer than Owen could remember. His only child had died at birth, along with its mother. Zach had helplessly watched her die and could never bring himself to put another woman through that jeopardy.

Riding toward the double cabin, Owen kept his eyes on the open dog run between its two sections. He shouted, "Hello the house. Anybody home?"

A gruff voice spoke behind him. "Turn slow, soldier, and show me who you are."

Owen turned quickly, stiffening at sight of a shotgun. Zachariah Danforth stood beside a small shed where he sheltered his harness, saddles and other goods that needed protection from the weather. He raised the shotgun to let Owen see the muzzle of it.

Owen swallowed. "Uncle Zach, it's me."

"Owen?" Suspicious eyes stared from under a wilted felt hat that had been old when Owen was yet a boy. "Come a little closer and let me see."

Owen was drawn thin, and he had not been able to shave himself decently since he had taken that saber wound. He wore a beard that had not felt scissors or razor since he had left the Georgia cotton warehouse that served as a field hospital. "It's me sure enough, Uncle Zach."

The eyes flickered with glad recognition, and the shotgun dropped to arm's length. "Git down, boy. I was lookin' for company, but you ain't what I expected."

Owen dismounted slowly, clinging to the saddle after his feet were on the ground, for his knees threatened to buckle. Zach was about to embrace him when he noticed the bound arm. He still almost broke Owen's right shoulder with a loving squeeze of his big hand. "You been hurt, boy."

"That's why they let me come home."

Zach's long silence and pained eyes spoke of sympathy. He had always provided a sympathetic refuge when

Owen had one of his many quarrels with his father. "I'll put your horse up and find him a bait of oats. You look like you've had a long trip on a bad road."

"Looks don't lie," Owen admitted, rueful at letting someone else take care of his horse. That was a job a whole man did for himself.

Relief washed over Owen as he stared into that kindly, beloved face. Zach was a little older than Owen's father, but the eyes were the same, the deeply lined face similar except for Zach's rough, gray-streaked beard.

"Good-lookin' bay you got," Zach commented. "Better than you left here on."

"Turncoat horse," Owen said. "He was in the Yankee army. I caught him runnin' loose after a little sashay against some Union supply wagons. Owner never showed up to claim him."

"Wonder the army let you come home with him. They keep the good ones for the officers and make the boys take the plugs."

Owen frowned. "A lieutenant taken him away from me. The night I left, I borrowed him back off of the picket line."

Zach spat. "I hope you brought home a gun, too. You'll need it, to keep that horse."

"There's a pistol in my saddlebag. I got it the same way I got the bay."

"Carry it in your pants, or in your boot. They won't give you time to fetch it out of your saddlebag."

Owen blinked. "Who? We never had much trouble with horse thieves in this country."

Zach gave him a troubled study. "Things ain't like you left them, son. You've probably got a notion you put the war behind you when you started back, but you didn't. It's here."

"Yankees?"

"Worse. The country's overrun with heel flies."

Heel flies were insects that buzzed around the hocks of cattle in season and drove them crazy. "What have heel flies got to do with the war?"

"These are the two-legged kind. Home guards, they call theirselves." Zach spat again, and Owen could see anger boil into his eyes. "They enforce the *con*script law and make sure everybody says a prayer once a day to Jefferson Davis. They see somethin' they want, they take it in the name of the Confederacy. They see somebody they don't like, they jail him for the same cause, or do worse. It's almost a pity you come home, boy. Now you'll see what you been fightin' for."

Before Texans had cast their votes for secession, Zach and Owen's father had been among several in the county who campaigned vigorously to remain within the Union. Sam Houston had talked against secession, and like many Texans those two old settlers thought Sam Houston had hung the moon. They had embraced the Union flag too long to turn against it.

That had been the source of much friction, some spoken and some swallowed, between Owen and his father.

He could see the years had not tempered Zach's feelings. He knew within reason that his father's would be as strong.

When the bay horse had been fed, Zach took Owen's rolled blanket and his saddlebags under his arm. "We tend the stock-first, *then* the men. I ain't got much in the way of fixin's, young'un, but I'll not leave you sleep hungry."

Owen might have been a *young'un* when he left home, but the war had whipped that out of him. Times he felt as old as Uncle Zach.

In the kitchen side of the double cabin, the old man coaxed a small blaze in the fireplace and hung a pot of beans to warm. He whipped up a batch of bread with stone-ground corn of his own raising and ground a double handful of coffee beans. "Coffee's scarce," he said. "I generally save it for Sundays, but this is an occasion." Lastly he cut thick slices of bacon and laid them in a skillet. It was simple bachelor fare, but to Owen it had the aroma of a feast in the making. He had missed more meals than he had found on the trail home.

Zach said with a touch of sadness, "It's good to have you here, Owen. Been an empty place without you comin' over to see me . . . you and your brothers."

An old ache came to Owen, and he stared at the floor. "I wrote you what happened to Ethan. Did you get my letter?"

Zach nodded. "Died in your arms, you said."

"It was quick. He was gone in a minute after the bullet struck him." He kept looking down, unable to lift his gaze. "I never did hear just what happened to Andy Jr., except that he was killed."

Zach was awhile in answering. He rubbed the corner of one eye. "It was after they started the *con*script law. Your daddy knowed they'd be comin' after your brother first thing, so he let him and a couple others of the same persuasion light out for Mexico. They got a hundred miles before a home guard patrol caught up to them. Claimed the boys put up a scrap, but you know Little Andy wasn't no fighter. Murdered all three and left them layin' where they fell."

Zach paused. "I went down with your daddy to bring the boys home, but some kind folks had buried them. We never could find just where."

Owen felt a biting anger and the helplessnes of loss.

"Dad shouldn't've let him go. If he hadn't been so almighty set against the war . . ."

Zach's eyes gave no quarter. "You taken one brother to war with you and lost him. Your daddy tried to keep the other at home and lost *him* too. Looks to me like you and him ought to call it even and find a way to get along."

Owen rubbed the hurting arm. "That's what I want to do, if he will."

"Give him time. They was brothers to *you*, but they was sons to *him*. You can lose a brother and go on. Lose a son, and you lose a part of yourself."

Owen said, "I'm not proud of the way I left here. I said things I shouldn't've. When I get home tomorrow, I'll set myself straight with Dad and with Mama."

Zach looked away, suddenly. "Your mama?" He gave his attention again to the cooking, turning the bacon with a fork. "I reckon where you been you didn't get much mail."

"Been way over a year since Mama's last letter. Most of the mail gets lost."

Zach set the food on the table. Owen tried to remember his manners, but the hunger was too much. He wolfed down the first plateful, then gave more time to the second. Zach ate little, watching him with troubled eyes. When Owen had finished, Zach said sadly, "I didn't want to tell you till you'd had your supper. Your mama died back in the winter. There was a fever come through the country."

Owen had seen so much of death on the battlegrounds that he had thought he was immune to grief, but this caught him unprepared. He walked outside, and Zach let him work out his feelings alone. Much later, when Owen went back into the cabin, Zach sat in an old rocking chair that had been his wife's. He looked at Owen without comment, waiting for Owen to speak. But Owen had no words to say.

Zach stood up, finally, and walked over to look at Owen's bandage. He unwrapped the dirty cloth and frowned at the wound. "Wonder you didn't lose the arm."

"Almost did. Truth is, Uncle Zach, they sent me home figurin' I stood a good chance to die."

"No money in your pocket. No medal on your coat. You didn't get much except experience, did you?"

"I've had aplenty of *that*."

Zach cleansed the wound with homemade whisky, which raised a fire in the raw flesh. He took a drink out of the jug and offered it to Owen. The fire in the arm was too strong for Owen to risk another in his belly.

Zach observed, "Still fevered some, I'd say."

Owen told him it was.

"Well, I know what'll draw that out. I'll fix you a pony poultice."

"A what?"

"You just set here and rest. I'll be back directly." Zach lighted a lantern and went outside. When he returned the aroma came through the door with him. He carried half-dried horse manure in a bucket. He said, "This won't do much for your social standin', but it'll do a right smart for your healin'."

He wrapped the arm lightly with clean white cloth, then applied a liberal helping of the manure and wrapped it over with more cloth to hold it in place. "I'll bet if you asked ten doctors, there wouldn't be *one* tell you about this."

"I expect not," Owen replied dryly.

The arm felt better; that Owen would have to admit,

though it was some time before he became reconciled to the odor.

He lay awake a long time, remembering his mother, seeing her face in the darkness, hearing her voice. It seemed to him that he could feel a drawing sensation in his arm, and a sense of extra heat even beyond the fever that had been in it. He slipped away finally into a heavy sleep demanded by his weariness. When he awoke, it was suddenly and in response to a loud voice.

"Danforth! You come out here, Zach Danforth, or we'll come in there and fetch you out!"

Owen sat up quickly, bringing a sharp pain to his arm. He blinked in confusion, not remembering for a moment where he was. He heard his uncle curse softly across the dark room as he dressed and stamped to get his feet all the way into his boots. Zach said, "You just as well get up, Owen. Night's over."

Owen was still putting on his clothes when Zach stepped through the cabin door and a presunrise glow was reflected in his bearded face. Owen let the left sleeve hang free, his heavily wrapped arm inside the shirt. He could hear a belligerent voice.

"We're lookin' for some deserters, Danforth. Tracks showed they was in the river bottoms yesterday. We figured you're the most likely man hereabouts to be hidin' them out. We're searchin' your place whether you like it or not."

"Go ahead and search, Shattuck, and God damn you to hell!"

Owen pulled on his boots and walked through the open door to stand beside his uncle. Against the half-blinding sunrise he saw a full dozen horsemen. He knew the one nearest the cabin. Before the war, Phineas Shattuck had been the kind of dramshop brawler who liked to beat up an occasional stranger smaller than himself but always slipped out the back door if someone bigger came in shopping for a fight. Owen's father and uncle had taken Shattuck to court over a wagonload of acorn-fattened shoats removed from the Danforth river bottom land. They had forced Shattuck to pay, but they had not gotten the man sent to jail as he had deserved. Shattuck was a landowner, even if a small and grubby one, and not to be lightly imprisoned like some luckless hired hand for becoming a little careless in the gathering of livestock. He was given the benefit of considerable doubt. Afterward, Andrew Danforth's barn had burned. Everyone knew who had done it.

Shattuck's hand went to the butt of a pistol in his waistband, and he glowered suspiciously at Owen. "Who are you?"

Owen knew Shattuck would feel no friendlier when he knew. "I'm Owen Danforth. Andrew Danforth is my father."

That name deepened the hostility. "What're you doin' here?" Shattuck stared at what was left of Owen's once-gray uniform. "You desert from the army?"

Owen touched his bad arm. "I taken a saber cut. They sent me home till I get well."

Shattuck seemed to believe, though it was plainly against his will. "You got any papers?"

"In the cabin, in my saddlebags."

Shattuck looked to the two horsemen nearest him. "Jones, Adcock, you go with him. Keep a sharp watch, and be sure there ain't nobody else in there."

Owen had given the other riders no more than a glance. When these two moved so he could see them without the rising sun in his eyes, he was surprised to find that they were boys, probably only fifteen or sixteen years old. One had the rough look of a born schoolyard bruiser. The other was unsure, perhaps even a little frightened. Most of the men from that age up to infirmity were gone to the war.

The older of the boys wrinkled his nose. "What stinks?"

Owen said, "My arm."

"My God," the boy declared, "you must've got the *gangrene.*"

Owen's saddlebags lay in a chair. His pistol was in one, but caution told him it was best they not see it. He opened the other and took out the paper he had been given, showing he was free to return home on convalescent leave. He tried to show it to the older boy, the rough one, who gave it only a glance, upside down, and said, "Captain Shattuck's the one to read it."

Captain Shattuck. A lot of rank, Owen thought, for a pig thief.

Shattuck read the paper without comment, then frowned at the two boys. "You look at the other side of the cabin while you're afoot. Make sure there ain't no deserters in it."

He shifted his attention back to Owen. "You sure you got a wounded arm? You sure that ain't just a lie to help you desert from the service?"

Owen held down a quick rise of anger. "You want to unwrap it and see?" He moved closer.

Shattuck's face twisted at the odor, and he backed off. "I'll be lookin' in on you from time to time. If you don't lose that arm, I want to be sure your old daddy and this renegade uncle don't make you forget you're still a soldier."

The two boys returned from the other side of the cabin and reported it clear. Shattuck said to Zach, "You probably got rid of them deserters before we come. We'll look the rest of the place over before we leave. If we ever catch you . . ." The rest went unspoken.

He rode to Zach's pens and observed the horses across the fence. "You, soldier boy, come over here."

Owen caught a half-trapped look in his uncle's eyes.

Shattuck demanded, "That big bay horse yours, boy?"

Owen said it was.

"A man on sick leave don't have use for a horse like that. We'll borry him from you and leave you one good enough for what little travel you'll be doin'. Adcock, turn that black horse of yours into the pen. I'll take the bay, and you can have mine."

Owen pushed forward to protest, but his uncle's restraining hand was firm on his shoulder.

The black horse was old enough to vote, almost, and seemed to favor its right forefoot. Small wonder, Owen thought darkly, that Shattuck wanted to force a trade.

"Come a long ways, ain't you, Shattuck?" he said.

"How's that?"

"You used to just steal *pigs*."

Shattuck drew back his big hand. Zach quickly stepped in front of Owen. "This boy's wounded, Shattuck."

Shattuck slowly lowered his hand, but the red did not drain from his face. "When you get ready to return to your regiment, soldier, I'll study about givin' this horse back to you."

He saddled the big bay and mounted. He ordered his men—his boys, actually—to spread out widely and sweep the field and pastureland all the way to the river. As they left, Zach said, "There'll be six foot of snow here on the Fourth of July before he lets you have that horse. The only way you'll get him is to take him."

"I'll do that," Owen swore.

Zach watched in silence until the line of horsemen disappeared over a rise and into timber along the river. "Well, boy, you've met the heel flies."

Owen looked at the black horse, the anger still churning. "I'd just as well saddle up and get started."

Zach shook his head. "Wait awhile. Give Shattuck and his boys time to clear the road."

Zach fixed breakfast, about the same as supper except that he did not heat the beans again. He ground more of his precious coffee beans against Owen's protest. Zach said, "We're kin, boy. What's mine is yours; you don't even need to ask. I'd always figured to leave this farm to you and your brothers. Now there ain't but you left. When I'm gone, the place belongs to you."

Warmth came over Owen. He wanted to hug his uncle, but he was shy about it. He could only say, "Please don't be in any hurry to go. I want you to live a hundred years."

"That's my intention."

Eating, Owen noticed Zach straighten suddenly. He asked, "They back?"

Zach motioned for him to hush and strained to listen. Owen heard some kind of birdcall. Zach pushed away from the table and walked out to stand in the open dog run. He looked around, then put two fingers in his mouth and whistled. Owen heard the distant birdcall again. The hair seemed to rise on his neck.

"Stand easy, young'un," Zach said calmly. "It's all right."

Four horsemen rode out of the timber on the river and up to the cabin. A young man looked vaguely familiar, a face dimly remembered from Owen's boyhood though he could not place name or circumstance to it.

The man was armed with two pistols on his belt and a rifle across his lap. He appeared severe enough to rush a bear with a willow switch. The other three wore gray uniforms, or pieces of them. Of late, the average Confederate soldier's uniform was whatever clothing he could beg, borrow or get away with.

Zach said, "Mornin', Vance Hubbard. Some fellers was here while ago lookin' for you and your friends."

Vance Hubbard. Owen remembered. Hubbard's father had been a farmer and a fellow campaigner with Andrew and Zach Danforth against secession. He had died, leaving a widow, a daughter and two sons. Hubbard studied Owen with as much suspicion as Shattuck had shown but without the malice.

Zach explained Owen's presence. Hubbard dismounted and extended his hand. Owen said, "I remember you now, Vance, but I had to look at you awhile."

Hubbard studied the stained and fading remnants of Owen's uniform. He said, "I hope your memory will continue to be just as short, should you be asked if you've seen anyone." A little of a smile came. "The time my father fell sick, your daddy and your Uncle Zach brought you and your brothers to help my brother Tyson and me bring in the crop."

Owen had not forgotten. "I was seventeen or eighteen."

"You did a man's work." Hubbard turned to Zach and nodded his chin at the three riders. "These men have hidden for two days without food."

"Anything I've got, they're welcome to."

Owen stood openmouthed. Zach explained, "There's a lot more people against this war than you might think. There's a bunch of men holed up in the big thicket over east . . . fellers runnin' from the *con*script law, and some who've taken French leave of the army. The heel flies ain't got the guts to try and root them out of that heavy timber. Vance and some of us do what we can to help."

Owen had heard nothing of this, where he had been.

Zach saw his consternation. "This ain't the only place, Owen. There's pockets of resistance like this all across Texas. Over on Bull Creek outside of Austin, a bunch of the boys are holed up in the cedar brakes just like these here. And out in the German settlements, there's a lot of Dutchmen dead set against Jeff Davis. They've kept troops busy almost ever since the war started."

Zach put his hand gently on Owen's shoulder. "Son, I know how you feel, so I wouldn't ask you to be a party to it. What say I saddle your horse and get you started to your daddy's place? What you don't see or hear, they can't hold against you."

Owen was uneasy, knowing these three men were deserters. By not reporting them he was putting himself in jeopardy, even bordering on treason. But he saw something in Vance Hubbard's determined face that would stop a cavalry charge.

Uneasily he said, "Looks to me like a risky business, Uncle Zach. I wish you wasn't in it."

"Everybody serves, son, one side or the other . . ."

As Owen started to ride away, Hubbard said, "Tell your daddy I'll be by to see him one of these nights."

Owen remained uneasy, for he had a hunch that to associate with Hubbard in these times would be akin to sitting under a lone tree while the thunder and lightning played.

He felt a touch of resentment. Nobody had a right to put his uncle in that sort of danger . . . or his father.

Chapter 2

Before the cabin came into view, Owen rode upon thirty or so spotted beef cattle that wore the family's D Bar brand, and with them a brindle milk cow heavy in calf. She would be freshening soon, ready to go back into the milk pen. The sight of the cows loosed a tingling of eagerness for home. The black horse, he had decided, was not so much lame as simply aged. The unjust nature of the forced trade still rankled. That bay had been worth a dozen snides of this kind. Phineas Shattuck had probably rejoiced all the way to town.

Owen had removed Zach's odorous pony poultice and bathed himself in the chilling waters of a creek. If pressed, he would have to admit his uncle's treatment seemed to have drawn out some of the fever. But the smell had been intolerable.

He skirted the edge of a field in which he had unwillingly worked from the time he had been seven or eight years old. The sweat used to stream as he stolidly gripped a Georgia stock and followed an equally reluctant team of mules. He had left here hoping never to touch a plow handle again. Now he wished he had two good hands for the work.

The house was a double cabin, built like Uncle Zach's, its two sections sharing a common cypress-shingle roof. Inside the open dog run between them, a narrow set of stairs led up to a sleeping area where Owen had wrestled with his brothers for blankets.

The nearer Owen came to the house, the more he tried to spur faster movement out of the black horse. The spirit might have been willing, but the flesh would not be rushed. Owen's eye was drawn to the little family cemetery, fenced with flat stones his father had hauled down from an outcropping on the hill the winter after he had settled here. The firstborn had been placed in the ground after just two months of a struggling life. Two other children lay beside him, their grave markers mute testimony to the harshness of early Texas. Owen pulled the horse in that direction, for there would be one more marker now than when he had gone off to war.

His throat feeling swollen, he dismounted and opened the iron gate. He removed his hat and stared at the newly chiseled stone that said *Idella Danforth, Beloved Wife and Mother*. The stone seemed to dissolve into a blur, and he did not hear the footsteps behind him until a familiar voice said, "Owen?"

Turning, he saw his father. Andrew Danforth looked ten years older than when Owen had last seen him. But he was still a towering figure, taller than Owen, even broader of shoulder because he had spent a long life at hard labor.

Owen wanted to go to his father and hug him, but

he could not. Andrew Danforth had the same reticence. He stood off at two paces and stared at Owen's bound arm. "It's not . . ."

"I've still got it," Owen said. "I just don't know yet how much use it'll ever be."

"Why didn't you ever write, son?"

"I did. I guess the mail never got through."

The elder Danforth looked as if he wanted to take the long step that would carry him to his son, and Owen waited for him to do so. But the best the two men could bring themselves to do was to stand at arm's length and awkwardly shake hands. Andrew walked to the new grave and touched his hand gently to the tall stone. "You didn't know about *her?*"

"Not till yesterday. I stayed all night at Uncle Zach's."

"I know. Phineas Shattuck came by a while ago with his guards, braggin' and threatenin'." He frowned at the black horse, standing with all its weight on three feet, showing no inclination to go anywhere though the rein was but loosely draped around the iron gatepost. "Not much of a trade, was it?"

"Someday, some way, I'll get my horse back."

Andrew shook his head. "Phineas can't help bein' what he is. Most of what his family ever had, they stole. Nobody would pay much mind to him before the war. Now they've got to, and he's made the most of it."

He looked at Owen's arm again. "Phineas would probably give ten years of his life to have an honorable wound like that, if he didn't have to suffer for it. He probably resents the fact that *you* got it."

"If he went where I've been, he'd have his chance. How come he's *not* in the army?"

"He owns a little land and some cattle. That exempts him. And he knows things some authorities wouldn't want him to tell." Andrew turned away from his wife's gravestone and looked at those of his other children. "There's two missin'," he said quietly.

Owen swallowed, listening for blame. Andrew might not say it, but Owen felt it was there, just beneath the surface. He wished he were still at Uncle Zach's.

Andrew seemed to have trouble bringing out the words. "It's good to have you at home, son, even in this condition. But you'd just as well know before we ever speak on politics: I ain't changed a particle."

Owen said, "Neither have I. But this is home."

He wished he could speak an apology and hear one in return. But he saw the determined set of his father's shoulders and remembered why he had left in the first place.

They walked toward the house, Owen leading the horse. Owen said, "This place looks just like it did the day I left it."

"Time you've been home a day or two you'll know it's not. I run out of day before I run out of things that need doin'. I mortally miss your mama, son."

Owen frowned. "You sure takin' care of the place is all you been doin'?"

Andrew missed a step. "What do you mean?"

"I met Vance Hubbard over at Uncle Zach's. He said he'll be by to see you."

Andrew stopped. "You still a soldier, or did they turn you plumb loose?"

"I'm still a soldier. If I get well enough, I'm supposed to go back."

"Bein' a soldier, there's things you'll be better off not knowin'. If you didn't report them to the government you'd feel like a turncoat. If you did, you'd betray old friends. So if somethin' comes along you don't understand, don't try to. Go off by yourself and try not to see anything."

Uneasiness stirred in Owen. He could guess, from things he had seen at Zach's, what his father was trying to say without putting it into words. "Dad, you and Uncle Zach are sittin' in on a dangerous game."

Andrew looked across the field, the rolling prairie. His jaw was firmly set, "I came here an American, when Texas was still a republic. I worked as hard as anybody to see that we got ourselves into the Union. I didn't stop bein' an American because of a family fight."

"You think that's all it amounts to, just a family fight?"

"That's the meanest kind of fight there is. You ought to know that, as much as anybody."

Owen rested the next couple of days. Most of the fever left his arm. He suspected Zach's pony poultice had helped, but he did not repeat the treatment.

He did the chores that were possible one-handed, feeling a rising of guilt that he could not do more to help his father. He began unwrapping the heavy binding every day and trying to exercise the stiffened left arm. At first it would not move except when forced by his right hand. Then he was able to move it slightly when he put a strong will to the task. He could flex his fingers a bit, though he had little control.

"It's comin' back," he told his father hopefully.

Andrew did not smile. He did little smiling that Owen could see. "Keep workin' at it, but don't raise your hopes. It's a long fall to the ground when things don't work like you thought they would." A little of bitterness was in his voice.

They talked of many things, but some they avoided. Left unspoken were their opposing opinions about the war, which stood like a stone fence between them. Never mentioned were Owen's brothers, who had died far from home. If the conversation threatened to turn in that direction, one or the other would change the subject. Owen began to hope the war might simply leave them alone, and that fence might never have to be climbed.

But the war came to them anyway.

Upward of noon one day, Owen was awkwardly going about the cooking of dinner while his father plowed out a new stand of corn. He heard horses approaching, and he stepped into the open dog run. Across the green pasture came a dozen riders, bathed in the bright sunshine of a Texas spring. They might have been a pretty picture had Owen not recognized the big bay horse and the man riding him. Anger rising, he stepped out of the shadows and looked toward the fields. His father had seen. Andrew Danforth laid the Georgia stock over and strode through the newly cultivated corn toward the cabin. He reached there about the time the horsemen did.

Phineas Shattuck was the first to speak, directing his attention to Owen. "How's that arm, soldier? About ready to go back to duty?"

Owen grudgingly raised the bound arm as far as it would go. He said, "It's a ways from healed."

His glance swept the line of riders. They appeared to be the same young boys, pretty much, who had ridden with Shattuck the last time. The rough one, Adcock, had pulled his horse up almost even with Shattuck's, but he deferred to another man, an older one, astride a big sorrel that Owen thought might be the finest-looking horse he had ever seen. He compared his bay to that one and thought he would not mind a trade. But of course he would have to get the bay back first.

The man wore a black patch over one eye, and a

streak of white whiskers ran like a slash through his dark-brown beard. Owen suspected the beard was an effort to hide a scar. War scar, more than likely; there were plenty of them around.

The man rode closer to Owen. "How did you get the wound, soldier?"

"Yankee saber, sir." Owen had unconsciously added the *sir*. This man had a bearing that identified him as an officer, though Owen had to look hard before he saw the badge.

The man said, "I received mine from a Yankee shell that killed my horse and two men nearby. They said I was unfit for further duty. I trust they have not dismissed you so lightly?" The question had the harsh flavor of gall about it. Clearly, he had not willingly given up the fight.

Owen said, "I'll be goin' back if this arm heals proper."

The man gazed at Owen's father. "And if you do not allow yourself to be influenced unduly by those whose loyalties are not as strong as ours."

Andrew Danforth said firmly, "My son's old enough to make up his own mind, Chance. I'll not tell him what he should do."

Chance . . . *Chancellor*. Owen remembered. Claude Chancellor had been sheriff of this county when Texas seceded. It was said of him that he had read more books than any man in the county, even more than a school-teacher. He looked different now. The war, more than likely . . . the eye patch, the beard, the wounds seen and unseen. By the tiny badge Owen took it that he was sheriff again.

Chancellor said, "I remember you, Owen. You were working in your father's field the last time I saw you.

You are a man now, with a man's responsibilities. Ordinarily there is no one who holds more strongly than I to the biblical injunction that thou shalt honor thy father. In your case, continue to honor him, but I would advise you not to listen to him in matters of duty."

Owen made no reply. He stared at the face and that stern eye. Compared to Chancellor, Phineas Shattuck was a cur standing in the shadow of a gray wolf.

Chancellor spoke to Owen's father in a tone that reminded Owen of their old friendship. Not all things had fallen victim to the war. "You may not have heard, Andrew, but there was some shooting last night. A patrol came upon Vance Hubbard and some of his hideout people from the thicket. The youngest Hubbard boy was seen with them. They got away into the timber without anyone shot, so far as we know. But now there is a price on Tyson Hubbard's head, just as there has been on his brother's. And there will be a price on anyone who helps them."

Owen looked for his father's reaction, but whatever Andrew Danforth was feeling, he kept it bottled up.

Chancellor said, "I felt it only fair to warn you . . . once."

Andrew Danforth said evenly, "We all do our duty, Chance, as we see it."

Shattuck declared, "If I was you, Claude, I'd haul him in to jail right now. You know where his sympathies are at."

Chancellor gave Shattuck a quick glance that showed his annoyance at the uninvited suggestion, or perhaps at the familiar use of his given name. As sheriff, Chancellor once had arrested Shattuck on charges brought by Andrew and Zachariah Danforth. Owen suspected he did not relish riding with the man now, even in the service of the Confederacy.

Chancellor studied Owen's arm, then his face. "Andrew, your son seems to have acquitted himself well in the service of his country. The old can often learn much from the young. I would suggest you seek your son's counsel." He drew away.

Shattuck pulled around to follow him but stopped. A touch of malice was in his eyes. He patted the bay horse on the shoulder. "Soldier, this is quite a mount you've lent to your country's service."

By the time Owen thought of an adequate reply, the guard detail had ridden away. He turned to his father and declared, "Phineas Shattuck would mortally love to catch you at somethin' he could call treason."

"And I know some people who would mortally love to catch Phineas Shattuck over in the thickets, without all those wet-eared kids around to protect him."

"*You* been over in that thicket, Dad?"

"You askin' me as a son, or as a soldier?"

Owen pondered darkly. "I ain't askin' atall. I take back the question." He thought he knew the answer anyway. "That Shattuck's dangerous."

"Only if you turn your back on him. I try to see him before he sees me."

"I wish you'd try not to see Vance Hubbard at *all*. He's liable to get you killed."

"He's the son of an old friend. This trouble won't change that." He obviously did not want to continue the subject. "How long till dinner's ready?"

Owen told him it would be thirty minutes if he did not drop anything, an hour if he did.

Andrew said, "I'll go back to the field. Can't afford to be wastin' daylight."

That night, as was his custom after supper, Andrew took down the big Bible that had been a wedding gift long ago to him and Idella Danforth. He read awhile by lamplight, then went out onto the dog run to sit in a straight-backed chair and meditate in the coolness of the night. He did not say, and Owen never asked him, what he was thinking about . . . the Bible, the war, better days when the family had been together.

Owen sat beside him in silence, flexing his fingers, moving his bad arm up and down as far as he could. He could see a little improvement from one day to the next.

Andrew exclaimed, "Did you see that?"

Owen straightened, alarmed. "What?"

"A little glow of fire out yonder, at the edge of the timber. Somebody lighted a pipe, I think."

Owen frowned. "Your Unionist friends?"

"They'd know better. It's probably some of those home guard kids, come by to take a look at this place."

Dread began to build in Owen. "Maybe waitin' for your friends to show up."

Andrew grunted. "Son, I didn't mean for you to leave one war and find yourself in another."

"You don't *have* to be in this one."

"In a way, I'm a soldier like you are. I'll do what I can to help those who believe the way I do."

"Sooner or later they'll drive you to the thickets. Or maybe worse."

"I'm a hard man to kill. Those home guards are mostly just boys anyway."

Impatiently Owen said, "A *baby* can kill you if you put a gun in his hands. Give these boys a bad model to pattern after and they can be as dangerous as grown men. Maybe worse, because they haven't learned how

to think things through for themselves. They follow whoever hollers loudest."

"Like you and Ethan did, when you joined the army?"

That stung. Owen said, "I may've been a kid when I
went, but that seems like ten years ago. I know what I'm
doin' now."

Andrew nodded grimly. "So does your old daddy."

Nights, Owen made his bed where he had slept when
he was a boy, over the dog run. At first, because he was
used to the noise and midnight comings and goings of
the military, the relative quiet kept him uneasily awake.
His first few nights at home he lay for hours listening to
the stirrings of the creatures that moved in the darkness,
the birds that sang by starlight. He had to get used to
them all over again, as when he had been a child.

One night—he had no clear idea of the time—he
awakened to a sound that did not fit. He raised up on
one elbow and listened. It came again, a faint birdcall
that sounded like one he had heard at Zach's cabin.
Heartbeat quickening, he pulled on his trousers and
climbed carefully down the ladder, favoring his left arm.

He was not surprised to see his father standing in the
heavy shadows of the dog run, pulling his suspenders up
over shoulders covered by long underwear but not by a
shirt. Andrew said sternly, "If I was you, I'd climb back
up yonder."

Owen's voice was just as firm. "I'm not sleepy."

"I don't want you mixed up in this."

"I'm already mixed up in it, just bein' your son."

Andrew seemed inclined to argue further, but something moved in dark shadow by the corral. A cloud covered the moon, and two men hurried to the cabin. An
urgent voice asked, "Andrew?"

Andrew said, "Come up onto the dog run, Vance, where it's good and dark."

With Vance Hubbard was a young man about Owen's age. Another runaway from the army, Owen assumed.

Vance Hubbard grimly shook Andrew's hand and turned to face Owen. "Remember my brother Tyson?"

An old memory stirred. Owen had considered Tyson the boy as quarrelsome, trying to dominate. He was well into his twenties now and looked about as always. Owen felt the distrust in Tyson's long stare and did not extend his hand.

Vance Hubbard said, "Would you mind leavin' us, Owen? I've got to talk to your daddy."

Owen demanded, "You fixin' to get him into trouble?"

Andrew said sternly, "We're already in trouble. It started the day Texas threw in with Jeff Davis."

Owen pointed into the night. "There's liable to be some home guards out yonder. If they catch the Hubbards here . . ." He did not feel that he had to finish it.

Tyson Hubbard's voice was like a challenge. "We circled the place real good before we came in."

Vance Hubbard was more conciliatory. "I wouldn't put your daddy in danger."

"He's in danger just *knowin'* you." Owen did not intend the resentment to color his voice, but it had.

Andrew said with reproach, "The Hubbard family have always been our friends, son. You'll treat them with respect."

"And if they get you killed?"

"Lots of people are gettin' killed these days."

Hubbard studied Owen with concern. "It'd be better if you went somewhere and let me and your daddy talk."

"I think it might be better if I stayed."

Andrew said, "I don't agree with my son, but I trust him. What brings you-all here, Vance?"

"My mother, and my sister Lucy. The government's seized our farm since Tyson went on the list. The home guards taken our womenfolk to town."

Incredulously, Andrew asked, "To jail?"

"No, but they've put them in a little house at the edge of the settlement where they can watch them easier. Figure, I reckon, that me and Tyson'll come after them."

Andrew's voice was angry. "Holdin' them hostage. That sounds like somethin' Phineas Shattuck would think of. They been mistreated any?"

"Not that I know of. But sooner or later they're liable to be, just from frustration if nothin' else."

"What do you want me to do, Vance?"

"I've written a letter to my mother. Reckon you could get it to her someway?"

"I'll *find* a way."

Owen interrupted angrily. "You know what'll happen if they catch you tryin' to smuggle a letter in there . . . *his* letter?"

Firmly Andrew replied, "They've got no right to hold a man's family. Where's the letter, Vance?"

Hubbard took it from his shirt pocket. "I never wanted them in the thicket, but now I don't see any other way till we can smuggle them away from here someplace. They're in danger where they're at. I'm tellin' Mama to stay ready. Sometime in the next few nights we'll create a diversion. While the guards are distracted, we'll go get her and Lucy."

"You'll get somebody killed more than likely."

"You got any better ideas?"

Andrew shook his head. "I'll take her the letter. And

if there's anything else I can do to help . . ."

Hubbard said apologetically, "I wish I didn't have to put this on you, Andrew. I'm afraid to ask your brother Zach. He'd just wade in there bold as Lucifer, tellin' Shattuck to go to hell. He'd end up in jail, or dead. And all for nothin', because the guards'd get the letter."

Andrew nodded. "Just tell me what house they're in."

The Hubbards were gone as silently as they had come. Tyson had said almost nothing, but his eyes had bored into Owen the whole time he had been there. Owen shivered, and he realized it was not from the coolness of the spring night. He stood in silence with his father on the dog run. At length he said, "The people in town all know you. The minute you get in sight of that house, they'll be on you like chickens on a June bug."

"I promised him I'd go."

Owen clenched his right fist in anger and frustration. "You won't go. *I* will."

Andrew blinked in surprise. "You'd do that for Vance Hubbard?"

"Not for him, for *you*. You're the only daddy I've got."

Chapter 3

In the fading light of early evening Owen warily studied two boys slumped in boredom on straight-backed chairs behind the livery. Andrew had told him Phineas Shattuck had confiscated the barn and corrals for the keeping of the home guard mounts after Old Dad Wilson, the owner, left town hurriedly in the dark of a winter's night. Like Owen's father and uncle, he had campaigned against secession. Like Andy Jr., he had been overtaken and left where he was caught.

Owen sensed that the two boys were not stable swampers. They had probably been assigned to watch the house where the Hubbard boys' mother and sister had been placed. All the way to town he had devised reasons for visiting the women, excuses he could tell the guards. He had rejected each in its own turn, knowing no better was likely to emerge from a reluctant imagination not used to constructing lies. The longer he considered, the less he expected any story to be accepted. He wore a Confederate soldier's uniform—the badly worn remnants of it, anyway—and the people in that house were womenfolk of hunted Unionists at a time when it could be worth a person's life to be a bunch-quitter.

A sack suspended from Owen's saddle carried food-stuffs his father had packed—bacon, a ham from the near-empty smokehouse, shelled corn to grind for bread. Andrew Danforth had always shared with people in need, sometimes at the risk of putting himself in the same condition. Carrying food to the Hubbard women was explanation enough, in Andrew's view. Texans could understand compassion for women, even for women of the enemy.

Without explanation Andrew had put a jug of his brother Zach's corn whisky into the sack. Andrew never used it much himself except for medicinal purposes, and he was seldom sick.

Owen had asked with a frown, "That Mrs. Hubbard . . . she's not one of them women that hides and drinks, is she?"

He remembered how she had looked a few years ago. He would not have taken her for a secret sipper. Andrew had reacted with indignation that Owen could even harbor such a thought about a good woman. But he did not explain the jug. "It just may come in handy," he said. "A little corn whisky can answer a lot of questions."

Owen judged that the two boys by the stable were not long from their mothers' apron strings. They might not be difficult to fool, but he felt remorse even before he made the effort. He would never have thought he would one day mislead people of his own side to favor a scal-awag Unionist. He drew a deep breath and touched his heels gently to the old black horse's ribs, reining him toward the poor, slightly leaning frame shack that served as a house. He had seen slaves living in better.

He recalled the good, solid log house on the Hubbard farm the time he had gone there with his father and brothers to neighbor-help. The elder Hubbard had broken his leg just as he had begun harvesting his corn crop. A lot of other people had been there, turning an unfortunate accident into a celebration of human kindness. Now some of the men who had labored for Hubbard that long, hot day were enemies of his sons. Others were hiding with those sons in the thickets. More than a few had gone away to fight, and some would never come home.

Where Owen had been, up against the Yankee lines, he had not seen the rancorous divisions which had materialized here in Texas. Perhaps, he thought, it had existed but had not been obvious to a soldier focusing his attentions upon his own survival.

He had chosen to arrive in town at dusk to avoid attracting more attention than necessary. It had been easy to locate the house by Vance Hubbard's description. The authorities had brought the Hubbard women to the poorest end of Poverty Alley, just behind the livery barn and corrals.

Well, he reasoned, if Vance Hubbard had not made his choice to throw in his lot with deserters and the like, he would not be a fugitive, and his womenfolk would not be reduced to this. Given *his* own choice, Owen would not be here to help them. Many a poor Confederate war widow was probably faring worse.

He was fifty feet from the house when the two boys roused themselves from their lethargy and swaggered out to meet him. He recognized the freckle-faced Adcock, who appeared to have assumed the leadership whether assigned it or not.

"Where you goin', soldier?" Adcock demanded. He would probably be a sergeant if he were a few years older, Owen thought darkly, and no credit to the rank. He had all the scars of the town's junior bully.

"I come to fetch some vittles to the Hubbard women," Owen replied.

The boy grunted his disapproval. "Don't you know who they are? A soldier like you, wounded and all, I wouldn't think you'd want no truck with the likes of them."

"I been fightin' against men, not against women-folks. Mrs. Hubbard was a nice lady before the war. I'd hate to think she was hungry."

"She won't go hungry," Adcock retorted. "We figure the first real dark night that comes along, them sons of hers'll be in to try and fetch her. Then we'll have them." His eyes narrowed. "Or maybe you wasn't really thinkin' about the old lady Hubbard atall. Maybe you was thinkin' about that girl." He quickly convinced himself and broke into a secret-sharing grin. "You been a long time away from the women, I expect."

Owen considered all the lies he had made up and discarded. Now this brash kid guard had furnished him one better than his own. He said truthfully, "I don't hardly remember her."

Adcock clearly did not believe that. The grin remained. "She's skinnier'n I like them, but I reckon she'd look good to a man who's been off to war awhile. We got to search you first. Orders from Captain Shattuck."

Captain, Owen thought sourly. The title still struck him as damned important for a pig thief.

The two boys went over him thoroughly, even feeling

his boot tops for a possible weapon. Owen had purposely left his pistol at home. He would have lost it here, had he brought it. He felt a little anxiety that they might discover the letter. Adcock rammed his hand deeply into the sack of grub. His face lighted as he lifted out the jug.

"I'll swun, soldier, you *must've* figured on havin' yourself a time. We'll have to hold this. Contraband, you know."

Owen realized why his father had put in the jug. He felt disappointment in the two boys, for they were much too young to be drinking the kind of liquid fire Uncle Zach cooked up. He asked, "Can I have it back afterward?"

Adcock exchanged a gleeful look with the other boy, probably not a day over fifteen. "If there's any left. Go on, soldier. Them women are welcome to the rest of the stuff, but this is too good for any scalawag family."

Adcock uncorked the jug. Owen led the black horse the short distance to the house, which had not even a fence to prevent loose livestock from wandering up onto the tiny porch. He tied the reins to a splintered hitching post which leaned to the south. As he lifted the sack of grub with his good arm he heard the younger boy begging Adcock to share the jug. Adcock kept turning away, denying him a drink. Owen frowned. He judged that Adcock would be flat on his back in a little while. The boy sure needed better raising.

Owen stepped onto the porch, which was barely large enough to sleep a respectable dog. Damned poor trade the government had made the Hubbards. Maybe when the next war came they would be a little more thoughtful about their loyalties. He rapped his knuckles against the doorjamb, not entering unbidden though the door stood open for the evening breeze to pass through. "Mrs. Hubbard?"

A girl moved cautiously into the doorway between front room and back. She stopped there, apprehension in her eyes as she blinked, trying for recognition in the poor light. "Who is it? What do you want?"

"Name's Owen Danforth. My dad thought you-all might be shy of vittles. I brought some."

The girl took a tentative step into the room. Her apprehension eased, suspicion taking its place. "You got a soldier suit on. You sure you're a Danforth? Maybe you just come here to spy on us."

Owen was about to tell her of the letter but heard a commotion behind him. The two boys were moving toward the house and wrestling over the jug. They seated themselves on the edge of the porch, Adcock laughing loudly and the other boy protesting that he was not getting his share.

The girl said testily, "I wish you'd tell your friends to go away and leave us alone."

"They're not my friends," Owen told her. It occurred to him that he probably had few friends in this town anymore. Most anywhere near his age had gone off to fight or had fled the country to keep from fighting.

In the fading light he realized he would not have recognized Lucy Hubbard if he had encountered her unaware. He remembered a shy and sun-blistered farm girl of fourteen or fifteen, possessing nothing in the way of looks that would cause him to think about her twice. Now she was grown, or just about. She still looked sun-blistered, probably having done a man's fieldwork since her father's death. She had otherwise turned into a presentable young woman, even *if* a little skinny. Self-consciously he asked, "Ain't your mother here?"

He heard a rattle of pans in the kitchen. Mrs. Hubbard said, "Who is it, Lucy?" and came into the doorway. He remembered thinking her a strikingly handsome woman the time he had helped harvest the Hubbard field. She looked older now. It seemed to him that everyone had aged more than the few years gave call for. "You're really Owen Danforth?" she asked, incredulous. "You've changed."

"Seems to be an epidemic of that," he remarked.

She looked with sympathy at his bound arm. "You're hurt."

Her concern left him flustered. It would be easier to dislike her if she didn't give a damn. "It'll be all right."

"I heard you mention your father."

"He sent some vittles. Heard you-all was taken from your home kind of sudden. He was afraid you might be needful."

Mrs. Hubbard smiled gratefully. "Andrew Danforth was always a kind man. But how did he know about us?"

Owen looked cautiously back toward the porch. He carried the sack into the poor, small kitchen and said in a low voice, "Your sons come by the place last night." He reached deep into the binding on his left arm and brought forth the letter. "Vance wanted Dad to fetch you this."

Mrs. Hubbard glanced at her daughter, then seized the letter. Owen quickly motioned her back toward the small fireplace, away from the door. "Them boys find out about this, I'll go to jail. And maybe you-all with me."

Lucy Hubbard stared at Owen with disbelief. "You're one of Jeff Davis's soldiers. How come you to bring us that letter?"

Owen's pent-up resentment edged into his voice. "If I hadn't, my dad would've. They'd've searched him better than they searched me. No tellin' what they'd've done to him."

"So you did this for him. You don't really care about *us.*"

Owen's face heated. "I didn't come here to lecture you about politics. I just come to fetch that letter."

Mrs. Hubbard said firmly, "Leave him alone, Lucy. He's run a risk to do us a favor, and I'm sure he had to search his soul."

Lucy replied stubbornly, "He's one of them. How do we know he didn't read the letter and tell Phineas Shattuck what's in it?"

Mrs. Hubbard studied Owen with patient eyes. "Because he's a Danforth. The Danforths have always been honorable people." She handed her daughter the letter.

Lucy's eyes widened as she read. "If they come and try to rescue us from this place, there'll be somebody killed."

Her mother raised a finger to her lips and looked quickly through the door toward the boys on the porch. Adcock lay on his back, humming softly. The other boy finally had the jug. From the level to which he raised it, Owen judged that the better part had been put to use.

"I'd best go," he said. "The less I know, the better for all of us."

"Please don't hurry," Mrs. Hubbard said earnestly. "I apologize for Lucy. This has all been hard on her. She had no part in it, but she's paid the same price as Vance and Tyson and me."

He would have felt more sympathy for the girl if she appeared to want any of it. "War ain't easy on nobody." He touched his left arm, for it had begun to ache. The long ride into town, he supposed. He moved toward the door.

Mrs. Hubbard caught his good arm. "You must be hungry. It'd be a poor show of gratitude if we let you leave without feedin' you."

He lied, "I ain't hungry. I don't eat much." He felt as if he were in some alien place. He wanted to get away from it and these women who represented the enemy. But the promise of food stayed him.

Mrs. Hubbard paid no noticeable attention to his answer. She emptied the sack Owen had brought. "Slice off some of that ham, Lucy. I'll fix up some cornbread. I don't imagine you've eaten too well where you've been, Owen."

Argument was useless. The welcome aroma of the cooking soon broke any harbored resistance. He went into the backyard to a small woodpile, miserable leavings of the house's last tenant. He could not swing an ax with one arm, but he could carry firewood a few pieces at a time. He dumped it into a wooden box beside the fireplace. He remembered that on the farm the Hubbards had had a big iron stove, where Mrs. Hubbard had cooked as well as Owen's own mother.

"That'll be good enough to finish supper," Mrs. Hubbard said.

"I'd just as leave fill the woodbox, anyway."

She shook her head. "We may not stay around to use it."

His mouth tightened. Two women, afoot. He could not see that they had any choice.

It was good dark outside when he sat down by dim lamplight to the ham and cornbread and brown gravy. There evidently was no coffee in the house. At her mother's bidding Lucy brought water in a bucket from

the cistern. She watched Owen with distrust. He recip-
rocated her feeling, but when she moved up beside him
to place a tin cup by his plate he sensed her body
warmth. It set him to tingling in a pleasantly uncomfortable way he had not experienced in a long time. He
tried the water and thought it had a slight flavor of cy-
press shingles.

Mrs. Hubbard studied him thoughtfully. When he had
finished supper she said, "You've done us a great service,
Owen. I hate to impose on you for more."

Suspicion arose quickly. "What more?"

"As long as Lucy and I are kept prisoners here we're
a danger to Vance and the others with him. Shattuck
wants him to ride in and try a rescue. That's why we
were put here—bait."

Owen nodded. "It looks that way to me."

"They've just kept a couple of boys posted through
the daytime . . . don't expect Vance to try anything in
the daylight, I suppose. But pretty soon they'll send a
heavier guard to watch this place all night. Those boys
appear to be dead drunk and asleep on the porch. If
we're to get away, now is the time."

"You might get clear of the house. But then what?"

"We'll manage. I'd take it as a great favor, Owen, if
you'd look around and make sure there aren't any more
guards outside."

"Mrs. Hubbard, I'm a soldier . . ." The look of hope
in her face stopped him. His father would have helped
her. He would probably still try, when he heard about
this. "All right," Owen said reluctantly. "I reckon I can
do that much."

Lucy protested, "He'll call up the guards, is all he'll
do."

Owen frowned at her. She was not making this any easier.

"Hush, Lucy," her mother said. "Sometimes you have to trust."

Owen walked out onto the porch. The two boys were as still as they would ever be, short of death. The jug lay between them, tipped over, the stopper out. Owen stepped farther into the street, making a long, careful survey. He returned to the house, still watching the sleeping boys.

He told Mrs. Hubbard, "Nobody out there that I can see. But they won't leave boys here long to do men's work."

Mrs. Hubbard looked to her daughter. In moments they had thrown together the few clothes they owned, tying them up in a tablecloth. They had sacked their little bit of food. She said, "Then we'd better not waste time."

Owen protested, "You won't get anywhere afoot. They'll catch you, come daylight."

Mrs. Hubbard said, "We know that. But the guards' horses are in that corral over yonder. We'll borrow a couple."

"*Steal*, you mean. You women don't know nothin' about stealin' horses."

"Do *you*?" Lucy challenged.

He had taken back his good bay horse from the officer who had confiscated it, but he did not consider that stealing. "I know two women ain't just goin' to walk in there and take two horses out of that corral."

"It's a risk," Mrs. Hubbard acknowledged. "But I see no other way." She had the hell-bent look of a drill sergeant.

He chewed his lip in anger, certain they would be

caught and that letter found. It wouldn't take the authorities long to realize who had carried it to them. He said, "You-all blow out that lamp, then, and come with me. I'll probably get hung if they catch me, but I couldn't go back and tell my dad I left you in a trap like this."

He gave the two boys another cautious glance as the women followed him across the narrow porch. Not even Gabriel's horn would awaken those heel flies before daylight. His pulse picked up while he moved briskly in the hoof-softened street, leading his black horse so he would not have to come back and get him. He felt that his heart was making enough noise to arouse the guard troop.

The women pressed close behind him. He could hear their footsteps, light and quick. He stopped at the corral gate and felt for the chain latch, careful not to make a noise. He handed the black's reins to Mrs. Hubbard with a silent command to wait. He studied the pen from one end to the other for sign of a guard. He rough-counted a dozen or fifteen horses. Several saddles had been placed upon the top rail, blankets draped across them, bridles hanging. Owen took short, shallow breaths, expecting at any moment to be challenged. He decided no one had seen reason to post a special guard on the horses in the friendly environment of the town.

Lifting a bridle from a saddle, he eased among the horses. Most drew away from him, but he managed to tempt one by extending his hand as if he held some sugar or a biscuit. Somebody's pet, he thought. He bridled that horse and led it through the gate to the women. While they quietly saddled it, he moved back among the horses with a second bridle.

He recognized the Yankee bay which Shattuck had

confiscated. Temptation almost overcame him. He thought of leaving the black in trade, but any such swap would be like painting his name in big red letters on the fence. He took another horse instead.

He half expected someone to raise a holler, and the hair seemed to bristle on his neck as the women finished the saddling. He wondered how they were going to ride astride with long skirts better suited to sidesaddles. Lucy Hubbard mounted first, her skirt pulling up. He tried not to look, but he glimpsed an ankle, more than a man was usually privileged to see, short of matrimony. Silently he reproached himself. This was no time to be letting his mind stray into such a direction.

Mrs. Hubbard appeared much calmer than Owen felt. She pointed her chin. "We'll ride yonderway till we're clear of town. We wouldn't want to run into anybody."

Irritably Owen demanded, "You-all know where you're goin'?"

"To your Uncle Zach's. He'll help us."

Owen said, "There's a chance they got people watchin' him."

Mrs. Hubbard showed no fear. "In that case we'll just have to take care of ourselves."

Owen tried to remember how she used to be. He had considered her a typical farm wife, handsomer than the garden run but otherwise not particularly different from most others he knew. She had seemed placid, accepting life as it came, even the time her husband broke his leg and could not harvest his crop. Owen did not recall seeing her show this kind of stubbornness before. "Even if they don't catch you—which they will—do you think you could find your way to the thickets all by yourselves?"

"We'll manage. You've done more than your part, Owen. You'd best be goin' home."

And spend the rest of his life explaining to his father, and to himself, why he had gone off and left two strong-headed women who needed help even if they didn't believe it . . .

"Damn it," he said, "I'll see you to Uncle Zach's."

Mrs. Hubbard did not argue. Owen glanced at Lucy and found her trying to pull her skirt down.

They rode in silence for possibly half an hour. Owen frequently looked back, listening for pursuit. At first he heard only the night birds and the nocturnal insects seeking to mate or to feed. He began to hope that he and the women had traveled far enough to evade any pursuit. Then he heard horses moving in a long trot, somewhere behind.

Grimly he said, "Must've found them boys on your porch." He reined toward the dark shape of a brushy motte. He dismounted and led the women into the dark shadows.

The black tried to nicker, and Owen held a hand over its nose. He would have been tempted to smother it had he not needed it so badly. The two he had taken for the women showed little interest in the oncoming horses.

His heartbeat quickening, he wished he could arrange for Phineas Shattuck to be forced to eat this black horse, raw.

He held his breath as the riders hurried along a wagon road that skirted the motte. When they were safely past he said, "Looks like they're headed toward Uncle Zach's. Probably outguessed you. You don't want to go there now."

Mrs. Hubbard shook her head. "We'll just have to

make the thickets. We'll find Vance and Tyson the best
way we can."

Owen grimaced, suspecting the answer before he
asked. "Think you know how to get to the thickets from
here?"

Mrs. Hubbard said, "They're northeast. Which way's
northeast?"

Owen grunted in frustration. "You don't know?"

"Clouds have got the stars covered up. I can't tell in
the dark, without stars."

"Then you're bound to ride in a circle till daylight.
They'll find you and fetch you back to town."

"Some soldiers carry a compass, Owen. I don't suppose you'd have one?"

He had never owned a compass or even had his hands
on one more than a time or two. He had been blessed
with a tolerable sense of direction as far back as he could
remember.

Angrily he said, "If I'd known how helpless you-all
were goin' to be, I'd've delivered that letter and been
gone like a shot. Now if they catch you they'll know
damn well I was the one got you out of town."

Lucy said, "Looks to me like you're bogged to the
hubs just like we are." Owen thought he detected some
sense of satisfaction in her tone. Despite his helping her,
she still resented the color of his threadbare uniform.

"But I ain't no runaway," he retorted.

"Not until now."

Mrs. Hubbard admonished her daughter to silence.
"Just show me the direction, Owen. If we get started
right, I think we can stay with it."

"No you wouldn't," he clipped. "You'd go around in
circles, like I said. You-all just let me alone to think."

He turned his back on them in irritation. Angry words

rose up but were denied expression by a control hammered into him by his stern upbringing. His sense of their having used him did nothing to cool his anger.

"I betrayed my government, just comin' to you-all in the first place. I've stolen government horses for you, and I've sneaked you out of town. They can't hang me but once. I'd just as well go the whole way."

Mrs. Hubbard said, "You don't have to, Owen." But her voice told him she wished he would.

"I'll take you to the edge of the deep thicket. After that, you're on your own."

Lucy Hubbard gave him the first completely civil words he had heard from her. "That's more than we could ever have asked."

Owen sniffed. He suspected this was what they had had in mind from the beginning. He rode in silence, ignoring them when they tried to coax him into conversation. Two or three times Lucy rode close enough to bump her leg against his. He wondered if she was trying to tempt him over to the Unionist side of the fence. It would be a cold night in July . . .

He stopped every now and again to listen, half expecting to hard-luck upon a detail of home guards. He began to fear that daylight would catch them still out in the open. As dawn's first glow began in the east, they reached the first scrub timber that marked the fringe of the dark and forbidding thickets.

He shifted in the saddle and looked behind him. Morning light was not yet strong enough to tell him whether what he saw in the distance might be trees or cattle or horsemen. He thought it prudent to assume the worst.

"We'd better ride into the brush a ways."

They moved perhaps half a mile into the closely

grown timber. The heavy growth made passage slow and difficult, briars tugging, Spanish moss hanging down and brushing his face. In a spot clearer than most he said, "The horses need a rest." He dismounted stiffly and loosened the girth so the black could breathe easily. He supposed he should help the women down, but he felt he had already gone the second mile and more. Once in a sortie he had been cut off behind enemy lines for a time. The same feeling of entrapment bore heavily upon him now as he experienced a sense of being in enemy country. He shivered to a chill that had nothing to do with the morning's coolness.

Mrs. Hubbard said, "You've done more than your due, Owen. We can tell our directions now. We'll ride till we come across somebody. We're bound to, sooner or later."

Owen nodded, dull from fatigue. "Sounds fine to me." He would be tickled to be shed of them.

He stretched out on the ground, gripping the aching left arm. The long night's ride had done it no good, and it had not helped the old black horse either. He drifted off into sleep.

He awakened suddenly as something sharp prodded his ribs.

A man stood over him with a long saber in his hand. "Wake up, soldier, and give an account of yourself."

Chapter 4

Owen decided against rising immediately to his feet. The saber point was near his throat. He did not know whether the red-bearded man threatening him was one of the thickets' hideout people or a home guard. He thought darkly that in his awkward situation it might not make much difference.

"I'm Owen Danforth," he said cautiously, raising his right hand to show he offered no resistance.

"Name don't mean nothin' to me," the man said brittlely. "You've got a uniform on. You run off from the army?"

"No. I was sent home till my arm heals up."

"Then you still fancy yourself a soldier?"

Owen suspected his reply was not the one this man wanted to hear, but he would not lie. "I'll be goin' back when I'm able."

The man moved aside one step, and Owen raised up

cautiously to a sitting position. He saw two men on horses in the nearby brush. One held the reins to the bearded man's animal. He betrayed no evidence of being any friendlier than Red Beard. Guardedly Owen said, "I brought these women to the thicket."

Mrs. Hubbard and Lucy had slept a little apart from Owen, in their clothes. The voices had awakened them. Mrs. Hubbard hurried to Owen's defense. "What he says is the truth. I'm Vance Hubbard's mother."

The man looked at her in surprise and tipped his hat. He took another uncertain step away from Owen. "Ma'am, it's an honor to make your acquaintance." He regarded Owen with unrelieved suspicion but nodded at him to get up. "I wonder at you, ma'am, bringin' this soldier with you. He's got no business here unless he's quit the army, and he says he ain't."

"We needed him."

"It don't seem likely he'd bring you out of kindness and him a soldier. Could be the government sent him to spy on us."

Mrs. Hubbard shook her head. "He was reluctant. I'm afraid we crowded him into it." Evidently more for Owen's sake than to convince the man with the saber, she added, "I hated to do this to him. But I saw no other way for my daughter and me to join my sons."

Owen slowly and carefully pushed to his feet. "Mister, if you're worried about me tellin' what I've seen, I ain't seen *nothin'*. What *is* there to see in all this brush? Times, a man can't hardly make out his horse's ears."

One man grinned, but the Red Beard stared coldly at him.

Owen argued, "This is the farthest I've ever been into the thickets. I expect the home guards've been farther."

The horseman with the grin pushed in closer. He said,

"Ain't been but a couple had the nerve to try. Some jolly boys marked their hides with a bullwhip all the way out. They ever come in here, it'll have to be with a big force."

Red Beard's eyes narrowed. "You might be the lad who fancies showin' that force the way in."

Owen's pulse was drumming. "I don't *know* the way in."

The bearded man turned to the two on horseback. "With all due respect to the ladies, I don't see how we can afford to let him go." He rubbed the butt of a pistol in his waistband.

Mrs. Hubbard interjected fearfully, "I've known this young man for years. His father is Andrew Danforth. He's helped many of the men who are in these thickets. Probably even you, Red Upjohn. I got his son into this predicament, and I'll take the responsibility for lettin' him go."

Upjohn said, "It ain't your responsibility to take, ma'am. It's mine." He turned a hard gaze on Owen. "We got too many lives at stake here to risk them for one. There's been good men shot or hung by the other side on nothin' but suspicion. And I'm *sure* suspicious of this one."

Owen saw madness in the man's eyes, and death. He could not breathe.

Mrs. Hubbard deliberately placed herself in front of Owen and spread her arms protectively. Lucy quickly followed suit. "If need be," Mrs. Hubbard declared, "we'll go back out with him. And if the home guards catch us, *you* can explain to my sons."

Red Beard looked to the other two men for support but found them against him. The one with the pleasant face said, "No, Red. We owe Vance too much."

"*I* don't owe him," Upjohn declared. "I found my way into this place without help, Banty Tillotson." He pointed the saber at Owen. "It was a soldier boy about like this one who put the rope around my son's neck and hung him before my eyes."

Mrs. Hubbard said, "Sir, killin' another father's innocent son won't put the breath back into yours."

The man called Banty placed a hand on the Red Beard's shoulder. "She's talkin' sense, Red. Come on now, let's take him to Vance and see what *he* says."

Red stared coldly at Owen. Owen's mouth was dry as he awaited the verdict. Red declared, "We dassn't take him in there. He'd see so much we *couldn't* let him go. Jim Carew, you stay here and watch him. Me and Banty'll take the womenfolks to Vance. Whatever he decides, I'll abide by it."

Mrs. Hubbard sighed in relief and turned to Owen. "I'll hurry things as much as I can."

Owen said urgently, "I've got to get home. If the guards go to our house and find me gone, they'll know. I'll be in trouble, and my dad with me."

Red Upjohn's eyes told him he was fortunate to have earned even this much of a concession.

Lucy touched Owen's hand. Her fingers felt cold. "I was unkind to you last night, Owen. I'm sorry."

His resentment arose again. "Sorry don't help much."

He sensed regret in her voice. "If your army is mad at you, you can stay in the thickets with us."

Owen gritted, "If my army finds out what I done, they'll be more than just mad. They'll probably want to hang me."

"You're makin' too much out of it. They can't really care that much what two women do."

"They care what your brothers do. And they care when somebody helps them."

He imagined he could still feel the gentle touch of Lucy's hand as she rode off into the brush with her mother and two of the men. She was still looking back at him as she quickly disappeared into the trees and scrub brush and briars.

Owen had never had reason to explore the dark, forbidding thicket country, even before the war. He knew the dense growth extended unbroken for miles. As a youngster he had been warned away by stories—probably untrue—of boys and even men who had sought to explore its mysteries and never came out. It was said a man could live in there for years if he learned its ways or become hopelessly lost and starve if he did not.

He silently took the measure of Jim Carew, a small man who deserved the nickname "Banty" more than the man who had it. Owen decided any lack of physical stature was offset by the rifle. It made Carew seven feet tall. Owen asked, "You quit the army?"

Carew eased. Even so, Owen had a notion he would shoot if pressed. "No. I taken my leave when I heard the *con*script men was comin'. They'd done taken my brother and let the Yankees shoot a leg off of him. Looks to me like you've paid *your* price. That arm goin' to stay crippled the rest of your life?"

"I'm beginnin' to get some use of the fingers."

"High price to pay for your slaves, don't you think?"

Owen replied sharply, "We never had no slaves."

"And neither does anybody else I know, hardly. Don't seem right for them to take us poor boys and make us fight so the rich men can have their slaves."

"It ain't just over slaves," Owen protested. "It's over rights and whether those people back east can tell us out here what we've got to do and all . . ." Owen stopped, anger rising. He realized he was falling back into an old quarrel he had lost to his father before he and Ethan had gone off to join the army. Argument with Andrew had been fruitless; why fire his blood again with a stranger? This was a dispute nobody ever won.

Owen said, "My dad sees things like you do. There's a good chance the guards are already at our place, tryin' to make him tell where I'm at. The longer I stay out, the worse trouble him and me'll be in. I wish you'd let me go home."

"And if it turns out you *are* a spy, and you bring the guards or the soldiers in here . . . I ain't takin' a thing like that on myself. So you lay down and get your rest, boy. If you're all right, you'll be home soon enough."

Owen assessed the determination in Carew's face and knew it was adequately reinforced by the power of that rifle. He lay down, but he did not sleep. Each time he opened his eyes just enough to see, he could tell Carew was becoming more and more relaxed. The man had probably stood guard all night. Owen made it a point not to move, not to jar Carew out of the lethargy into which he was slipping.

Carew's chin eased downward. He let his eyes close a moment, opening them suddenly and wildly as he resisted going to sleep. Owen lay still. Presently Carew nodded off again. This time he slumped. Owen waited to see if he might bestir himself, but he did not.

Cautiously Owen pushed to his feet. Standing over the sleeping man, he reached down and grasped the rifle. Carew's hand had opened and let go of it, but the weapon remained against the man's chest. Owen picked it up and stepped back.

Awakened, Carew grabbed at it but missed. He stared at Owen in dismay.

Owen said, "You just sit there. I got no interest in hurtin' you, and I got no interest in betrayin' your people. I just want to get back where I belong."

He tried in vain to think of some way he could saddle the black horse with one hand and not relinquish the rifle. He beckoned with his chin. "You'll have to saddle him for me."

Carew frowned. "I don't think I will. You don't look like the kind that'd shoot a man."

"I've shot at Yankees. Seems to me you're kind of a Yankee, bein' where you're at."

Carew made a step. "I don't think you'd shoot me."

"Maybe I'd just fire this thing into the air, and we'd see who comes first—your people or the home guards."

"All right," Carew grumbled, "I'll saddle him. But I'll catch hell when Red Upjohn gets back here with Vance Hubbard. And that grinnin' Banty Tillotson will hooraw me for a week."

Owen looked with some temptation at Carew's horse, a better-looking specimen than his own. He considered forcing a trade but feared the animal's description might be known to the authorities. It might even be stolen.

I'm in trouble enough already, he thought.

When Carew had finished, Owen swung into the saddle.

Carew complained, "I'm goin' to catch hell for sure."

"You want to come with me?"

"I ain't in *that* much trouble."

"I'll leave your rifle out yonder a ways." Owen touched heels to the black horse's ribs and sought his way through the tangle. He looked back two or three times, afraid Carew might be following, but he saw nothing. At the edge of the brush he paused, searching for a home guard patrol. He saw only a scattering of cows, quietly grazing in the morning sun.

He considered keeping the rifle, but he had made a promise. He wedged it into the fork of a hackberry tree.

He began to wonder if the pursuit had been only in his mind, a product of his fear and his feeling of guilt over helping the Unionists. That group of riders last night might have been nothing more than routine patrol. They might not even have been home guards; they could have been anybody.

A rising morning breeze moaned through the brush behind him. He was reminded that Hubbard's people in the thicket might bring him more trouble at the moment than anybody out in front. He rode across the open prairie in the direction of Zachariah Danforth's. Maybe Uncle Zach would feed him and advise him what he should do next.

A sense of caution bade him approach Zach's place from the timbered side, where he could see before he was seen. He tied the black horse and cautiously walked the last few feet to the edge, stopping in the shadow to survey the ground.

Dark smoke twisted where the cabin was supposed to be. The wind lifted it for a moment, and he saw to his horror that the cabin was down, its roof and part of the walls fallen in, still ablaze. He forgot caution in the rush of anxiety. He grabbed the reins and swung them up over the black horse's head, bumping his own head fiercely on a heavy, low-lying branch as he pushed himself up in the stirrup. "Uncle Zach!" he shouted as he spurred out of the timber, looking anxiously for sign of the man.

He saw him, lying facedown a few feet from the burning cabin. Zach's clothing smoldered from the heat of the blaze. Owen jumped to the ground. The black horse snorted and tried to jerk free of him, fearing the flames. Owen had to wrap the reins around his wrist to keep from losing him.

He knelt and touched his uncle, knowing even before he did that Zach Danforth was dead. He saw the bullet wounds, half a dozen at least. Any one of them would have been enough. Whoever did this had taken out a lot of spite.

Shattuck! It had to be Shattuck. Firing the cabin fitted his style, like the time he had burned Andrew Danforth's barn for revenge. Andrew had not been able to prove it, but he knew Shattuck had bragged about it to some of his cronies. That kind of talk was hard to keep secret, though it had no value in court.

One side of the cabin collapsed with a sudden rush of sparks and flame and smoke. The black horse jerked loose and trotted off twenty or thirty yards before stepping on the reins and stopping himself. Owen got his one good arm beneath his uncle and clumsily dragged him farther from the flames. He turned him over and tried to wipe the dried blood from the face and beard. He knelt then and cried, partly from grief, partly from rage.

Murdered him! Set the place afire and shot him when he came out. Shot him down and went off and left him.

Owen held to his uncle's hand and let the first outpouring run its course. He looked around for something with which to cover his uncle's body but saw nothing. Everything had burned with the cabin. He walked out to the black horse, untied his coat from behind the cantle and used that.

A thought struck him, and his jaw dropped in horror.

They'll be going for Dad . . . if they're not there already!

He swung up into the saddle, wishing for a weapon but having none. Anything Zach might have had was either stolen by those who had killed him or was destroyed by the blaze. His stomach churning, he turned for one more look at the place where he had known many happy times as a boy.

"Someday, Uncle Zach . . . some way . . ."

He saw the horsemen then, two of them, a quarter of a mile away and moving toward the smoking remains of the cabin. His heart tripped.

The distance was too great for him to tell if one might be Phineas Shattuck. He clenched his right fist but knew it would be foolhardy to remain here without a weapon. He moved the black horse quickly into the timber to be out of sight, and once in its cover he moved as rapidly as the dense growth would allow, in the general direction of home. He paused once to look back at the riders, to see if they might be in pursuit. They continued to move toward the cabin. Either they had not seen him or they had no interest in him. That, he thought, made it unlikely either was Shattuck. They might be other contingents of the home guards, however, or they might be Red Upjohn with Jim Carew or Banty Tillotson trailing him from the thicket. He had no desire to confront either possibility.

Impatience burned, but he forced himself to remain within the protection of the timber. In earlier years when he had fled a disagreement with his father, he had used this cover to take him to the sanctuary of Uncle Zach's. Zach had always had an easy knack for cooling tempers on both sides so that Owen and his father would ride home together in a spirit of reconciliation. But Zach had not so easily handled his *own* temper. The persuasive powers he used on others he had been unable to apply to himself. Owen could only speculate that some angry confrontation had preceded his uncle's killing. Phineas Shattuck would not have required much provocation, especially if he held all the advantage.

Owen moved occasionally to the edge of the timber to look for anyone following him, but he saw and heard no one. That only partially relieved his concern. It would not require much imagination for someone to guess he was following the course of the timber and to parallel him, just beyond sight on the rolling prairie.

Late in the afternoon he came to the homeplace, to a point from which Vance Hubbard had emerged that night to visit with Andrew Danforth. There Owen dismounted and walked to the edge, crouching. To his pleasant surprise he saw his father in the field, hoeing weeds from the growing corn. Owen watched briefly, hardly able to believe that Shattuck and his guards had not already come to take Andrew into custody, or to do what they had done at Zach's.

Perhaps, then, there was still time.

Owen remounted and rode out of the timber. His father saw him and leaned on the hoe, relief coming like sunshine into his furrowed face.

"Son," Andrew spoke gladly. "I'd about decided they'd taken you. Come dark I was fixin' to ride to town and see. Where the hell you been?"

"I'll tell you directly," Owen said urgently. "Right now we've got to get away from this place, while there's still time."

Andrew blinked. "Time for what? They didn't catch you, or you wouldn't be here."

Owen's right hand clenched into a fist. "There's no easy way to tell you, Dad. They've killed Uncle Zach."

Andrew sagged as if Owen had hit him. He let the hoe fall. His lips formed the word, "Zach," but Owen did not hear it.

Owen said, "Somebody shot him. Burned the cabin. Shattuck, I'd guess. I thought he'd've been here for you before now."

Andrew's big knuckles went almost white as his hands made powerful fists. "They wouldn't just've shot him without some excuse . . ."

"I helped Miz Hubbard and her daughter get away from town last night. I taken them to the thicket. Shattuck probably figured Uncle Zach had a hand in it. I just can't figure why he hasn't already been *here*."

Andrew stiffened, his gaze hardening on the line of timber down by the river. "I reckon he has. He was just waitin' for you to show up."

Owen turned quickly in the saddle. He heard the heavy drumming of hooves as half a dozen horsemen spurred toward him and Andrew. At the head of the group rode Phineas Shattuck, on Owen's big Yankee bay. Even at the distance, Owen saw a pistol in his hand. He glanced at his father and saw that he carried no weapon.

"Swing up behind me, Dad. We'll make a run for it."

Andrew made no move except to shake his head. "Ridin' that old plug? They'd be on us like hornets. We'd just as well meet them here." His face clouded with outrage as his gaze fastened upon Shattuck.

Owen watched the riders come, and his heart sank. "I'm sorry, Dad. I knew better, all the time I was helpin' them women. One thing just led to another . . ."

"It was my fault for not leavin' you out of it. Just don't say nothin' to Shattuck. Act like you don't know nothin', and don't admit to nothin'."

Shattuck swung his arm. Some of the riders circled to surround the Danforths. Shattuck reined up, victory in his eyes. He held the pistol at arm's length, pointed at Owen's father. "Andrew Danforth," he declared with great solemnity, "I place you and your son under arrest in the name of the Confederate States of America. The charge is treason!"

The words were so careful and deliberate that Owen felt Shattuck must have rehearsed them over and over in his mind.

"Treason?" Andrew asked, his voice firm. "On what grounds?"

"On the grounds that you and your son plotted to aid and abet the escape of prisoners important to the government."

"Prisoners?" Andrew asked. "What prisoners?"

"Them Hubbard women. You knew damned well we was keepin' them in town to make Vance Hubbard show hisself. Your son here, this gallant wounded soldier . . ." his voice went harsh with sarcasm ". . . tempted two wet-eared boys with a jug of whisky and snuck them women out of town. Stole some horses, too."

Owen was about to speak, but his father moved up beside the black horse and leaned a shoulder heavily against Owen's leg. Owen remembered the admonition to hold silent.

Andrew said, "My son reluctantly took some food-stuffs to Mrs. Hubbard because I asked him to. If the women left town afterward, he wouldn't know nothin' about that. He come right on home."

Shattuck's eyes lighted on Owen with a savage triumph. "Your son's just now *got* home. We been watchin' this place for hours."

"He left again this mornin' early, to go see his Uncle Zach."

Owen marveled at the ease with which his father lied. He never used to have any inclination in that direction. The war, Owen decided. It made men lay aside old moralities and do whatever was expedient.

Doubt flickered briefly in Shattuck's face before conviction returned, and victory. "We was there this mornin'. We didn't see nothin' of him."

Andrew's voice hardened. "He got there after you'd gone. He found Zach just like you left him." Accusation burned in his eyes.

Shattuck's jaw dropped, but he regained his confidence, for he was the one holding the pistol. "We went to take your brother into custody. He put up an argument, and there wasn't no choice. He was shootin' at me."

Owen saw Shattuck's eyes waver. They said he lied. Owen looked at the young guards who sat their horses beside Shattuck. One was the freckled Adcock, who had been dead drunk when Owen had left him last night. One side of his face was blue and swollen. Somebody had struck him, hard. Adcock was hunched in the saddle as if in mortal misery, staring at the ground. That also told Owen that Shattuck lied. His stomach burned with hatred.

Andrew declared, "You've got no evidence, Shattuck. I say my son came home last night. You got any proof that he didn't?"

Shattuck leaned forward, bringing the pistol's muzzle up to point at Owen. "I know what he done. That's all I need."

Andrew declared, "A court'll want evidence."

"Court? Who said anything about a court?" He

turned to young Adcock. "You ain't much on brains, boy, but you can trot up yonder and catch a horse for the old man. Saddle him and get yourself back down here in a hurry. Johnson, you go with him. If he ever slows to a walk, I want you to use your quirt on him."

Despite his own predicament, Owen was able to feel sorrow for Adcock, and a touch of guilt. The boy might be a blusterer and a bully, but Owen had trapped him into this disgrace.

Owen soon had worry enough over his own predicament. As the two young guards led a saddled horse to the field, Andrew demanded, "You goin' to let us go to the house and pick up some clothes?"

Shattuck said, "Them you got on'll do fine."

"Not for long."

"You ain't *got* long."

Owen saw a grim conviction come into Andrew's face. Andrew gave his son a look that expressed regret he could not have put into words.

Owen knew, then, and he shuddered. Shattuck did not intend for them to reach town.

Chapter 5

Andrew Danforth grimly studied Shattuck, then his gaze drifted over the boys as if he harbored some forlorn wish for help from them. "You're talkin' murder."

"In a war there ain't no such thing as murder."

"My son's a Confederate soldier. He's not your enemy. Kill *him* and it's murder."

"Not when he's done treason."

Andrew gave his son a long look of regret, of silent apology. "Shattuck, treason has got nothin' to do with it. This is for revenge because we put the law on you years ago."

"So *you* say. I say you've both betrayed your country. We're takin' you to town. If you was to try and run, we'd have to shoot you."

Andrew's voice went hard with accusation. "And you'll say we ran, whether we do or not."

"You'll run. Sooner or later you'll see it's the only

chance you've got." He smiled coldly. "Take it *now*, if you want to."

Owen saw defeat in the slump of his father's shoulders. Sadly Andrew said, "I wish you hadn't come home, son."

Dread settled in Owen's stomach like something dead. The boy Adcock looked at him with eyes that told of shame.

Andrew said darkly, "Convenient for you, Shattuck. First Zach, then us . . . all three Danforths in one day."

Shattuck replied, "The fortunes of war."

"The war won't last forever. No matter which side wins, you won't always have the office to hide behind. Sooner or later *somebody*'ll get you. It's just a question of who."

Color surged into Shattuck's cheeks. "You shut up, Danforth, or I'll shoot you right here." He leveled his pistol.

Owen went rigid, expecting the blast.

One of the boys said, "Somebody's comin', Captain." His tone was of relief.

Shattuck's pistol swung around as his head jerked. Two riders skirted the Danforth cabin and moved down toward the field. Shattuck squinted, trying worriedly for recognition. "Who's that?" he demanded. "Who *is* it?"

The boy named Johnson replied, "Looks to me like Sheriff Chancellor."

Shattuck cursed under his breath. "Ain't he got nothin' better to do . . ."

The brown-bearded Chancellor and a younger man rode up in a brisk trot. The sheriff's eye fastened momentarily upon Owen, then upon his father and finally upon Phineas Shattuck. Owen tried to read whatever thought lay behind it, but the good eye betrayed no more secrets than the patch which covered the other. Chancellor said, "We were afraid we'd find these two like we found Zach. We have trailed you all day, Shattuck. Why didn't you let me know what happened in town last night?"

"It was *my* business and no concern of the county," Shattuck said defensively. "There was treason done. It was my place to set it right."

Frowning, the sheriff rubbed one hand along the side of his face, where a white streak through his beard covered a war scar. "Wilkes and I buried Zach in his family plot. How many times do you have to shoot a man to kill him?" Accusation was in his voice.

"You know what him and Andrew've been up to all along. And this boy here, he forgot what uniform he had on."

Chancellor gave Andrew a moment's study, Owen a bit longer. "Zach Danforth was a good man. He was a friend of mine once. I had hoped he would be again, when the war is over."

"He resisted arrest. I was forced to shoot him."

The sheriff turned to the boys for corroboration. None would look him in the eye. His frown deepened. "What's your evidence against these two?"

Shattuck straightened in the saddle as if bracing for attack. "I've got all the evidence I need, and it's not a county matter. We're takin' these traitors to town. You can go on about your business."

Chancellor gazed at him so sternly that Shattuck had to look away. "My business is in town. So long as you're traveling in that direction, we'll ride along and help you."

"We don't need no help."

"They might try to run away, and you would have to

shoot them. With a couple more of us to watch them, they won't run." A hard smile flickered as he glanced at his deputy. The deputy glared at Shattuck with no effort to hide his contempt. Chancellor turned his attention again to Owen. "Soldier, I don't want to believe you would do anything to disgrace that uniform."

Owen said, "I never had no such intention." He hoped his eyes did not betray a lingering of guilt for what he had done. He could lie to Shattuck as his father had, without hesitation or shame. Chancellor was another matter. That one eye seemed to pierce all pretense and seize mercilessly upon the truth.

Andrew pulled Chancellor's attention from Owen. "I'm glad you came along, Chance. I tried to tell Shattuck, but he wouldn't listen. You've got no argument with my son."

Chancellor looked again at Owen, but he made no commitment. "Shattuck, it will be way into the night before we get to town."

Tightly Shattuck said, "It's *Captain* Shattuck!"

"To these boys here, perhaps. I have a longer memory."

Shattuck colored again. "Johnson, lead out!"

Chancellor spoke quietly to his deputy, who positioned himself beside Andrew. Chancellor pulled his horse in by Owen's.

Owen saw his father bow his head and close his eyes. Offering up thanks, Owen thought. And well he might. As the fear ebbed, Owen's anger came back. Some was directed against his father. Andrew's partisanship had put them in this predicament. Texas was Confederate, not Union. If he and Zach could have accepted that . . .

Riding, Owen flexed the fingers of his left hand. They

were slow to respond, but at least they showed improvement.

The sheriff watched him. "Considering going back to your old unit?"

"I wish I was already there."

"I don't know how bad a mess you're in. It depends upon how much credence the court places in Shattuck."

"What if they believe him?"

"At the least, prison. At the worst, a rope. You'd better think hard about what you'll say for yourself, soldier."

"I'm loyal to Texas. This wounded arm ought to say that for me."

Chancellor gave him a long appraisal, then shook his head. "Half the men you meet today carry a battle scar."

Bitterly Owen said, "Show me Shattuck's."

The black horse felt as if it would collapse beneath him before they reached town. The animal had been ridden almost continuously for more than twenty-four hours with little time to rest and graze. But for Owen to say so would be to admit what he had done last night. He held his silence and pitied the old horse. It gave him no satisfaction to realize that the guards' horses had been through nearly the same punishment. The big Yankee bay seemed to hold up better than any. It was too good an animal for trash like Phineas Shattuck.

Owen felt relief of sorts when the lamps and lanterns of town began to glow through the darkness, though he knew well enough what awaited him there. They rode past the darkened little house from which he had taken the Hubbard women. The boy Adcock gazed at the place and mumbled darkly.

The jail was of rough lumber, old and sagging a little atop a foundation of heavy posts which held it up from

the ground. It had been built in the Spartan days of the
Texas republic when people were few and money
scarcer. Owen had considered it a misshapen structure
even when he had had no reason to fear it. Now it was
an ugly presence brooding in the darkness like some
fearful old fortress out of the Dark Ages in stories he had
read as a schoolboy.

Shattuck said, "Well, Chancellor, we've got them
here. There ain't no need you troublin' yourself any further."

His voice betrayed too much of hope. Owen looked
anxiously at the sheriff. Chancellor smiled with a raw
irony. "We've come this far. We had just as well see
them safely inside a cell. It might strike their fancy to
turn back at the door and run."

Owen sighed. He dreaded a cell, but that was safer
than being in the open with Shattuck if no outsider was
around to see.

Shattuck brusquely ordered the guards to dismount.
He dispatched half of them to lead the horses to the
corrals. "Adcock," he commanded, "I want you to brush
my horse real good. I want to see his hair shine like a
mirror when the sun comes up in the mornin'. You hear
me?"

Adcock replied in a small, angry voice, "Yes sir."

"See that you do, or I'll wear out a bullwhip on you."
He turned then to Andrew Danforth, shoving him
roughly through the door. "Git in there!" He turned
toward Owen, but Sheriff Chancellor positioned himself
between them.

Chancellor said, "Go ahead, soldier."

Owen stepped through the door. The inside was
pitch-dark. He could barely make out the form of his
father just in front of him. If there had been any way

out except the front door, this would be the time to break and run, he thought. But run where? He listened to the trampling of heavy boots as the rest of the men and boys crowded in behind him.

Shattuck demanded, "Where's that jailer? Why ain't there a lamp lit? Benson, damn you, where are you at?"

Someone struck a light and lifted the chimney from a lamp. Suddenly Owen became aware that more men were in the room than should be. Five or six more, at least. He heard Shattuck's gasp as someone shoved the muzzle of a big Navy revolver to his throat.

A stern voice ordered, "Everybody stand real still!" Owen knew that voice. He had heard it at Uncle Zach's and again at his father's cabin. A man moved into the narrow circle of dim lamplight, a pistol in his hand.

Vance Hubbard.

Hubbard's younger brother Tyson held the shuddering Shattuck at gunpoint. Red Upjohn and Jim Carew and the grinning man named Banty stood just at the edge of the lamplight.

A couple of guards who had made it only as far as the door turned to run away into the night. Owen heard a commotion outside and knew they had been stopped. Vance Hubbard evidently had brought a sizable contingent of the brush people to town.

Firmly but with some semblance of courtesy Hubbard said, "Chancellor, I want you and all these heel fly boys to go back yonder into that cell, where the jailkeeper is at. Real quiet now. I wouldn't want anybody to get hurt."

Chancellor, his hands raised, looked back at Shattuck. With sarcasm he said, "You've given the orders all day, Shattuck. What do you say now?"

Shattuck eyed a pitiless young Tyson Hubbard, whose

expression indicated that he would gladly squeeze the trigger. Shattuck rasped, "Do what he says." The guards moved into two open cells, as ordered. Shattuck started to follow them, but Tyson Hubbard stopped him, stroking the muzzle of the pistol against Shattuck's bobbing Adam's apple.

"Not you," he said. "We just might take you with us."

Shattuck's eyes went wild. "What're you fixin' to do?" No answer came. He asked again, fearfully, "What do you want me for?"

"To be sure nobody follows too close. If anything happens, they'll have to stop and bury you."

Shattuck made a noise as if he were strangling.

Andrew Danforth had been silent. Now he said, "You've taken a lot of risk, Vance."

Vance Hubbard closed the cell door on the men and locked it. "No more than you've done, many a time. I'm just sorry we didn't get to Zach's place in time. They killed him."

Andrew looked at Shattuck, and his eyes narrowed in hatred. "I know."

Hubbard said, "I was afraid even this might be too late. I thought Shattuck might never get to town with you."

Andrew said, "Claude Chancellor's to thank for that. He came along just when we needed him."

Hubbard looked through the cell door. "Chancellor, I wish we weren't on opposite sides."

Chancellor responded firmly, "We were not always, but we are now. The only thing that can change it would be for the war to end."

Hubbard signaled for his men to retreat outside. Owen was reluctant to move. "Where we goin'?" he demanded.

"Out to the thickets, amongst our own."

"*Your* own, not mine." Owen said. "I don't belong there."

Tyson put in, "You do now. After what you done for my mother and sister, you can't stay here."

Owen knew Chancellor and Shattuck had heard. Angrily he declared, "I *might've*, if you hadn't said anything. Now you've spoiled that for me."

Andrew gripped his son's right arm. "Come on, Owen, we ain't got time now to argue."

From the cell Chancellor said, "You'd *better* argue, soldier. Once you ride away with those people, you're an outlaw."

Owen protested, "I didn't ask for this." He looked to his father. "Dad, it's already gone too far . . ."

He did not see the fist coming until too late. His head rocked back under the force of his father's hard knuckles, and fire exploded in his eyes. He fell. Strong arms caught and lifted him. He heard his father's voice, dimly. "Sorry, son, but we'll argue later. This ain't a fit time to talk."

He felt himself supported between two men, his feet dragging. His head pounded; his jaw ached. He struggled to pull free but was too weak to fight. He was aware that they were at the livery stable, and he heard his father say, "Put him on that big bay horse Shattuck was ridin'. It's rightfully his."

Red Upjohn argued that the horse was sweaty and tired, but Andrew said it was not that far to the thickets. The horse would have plenty of time afterward for rest. Owen was lifted into the saddle. When he felt himself about to slide off, somebody grabbed him. Vance Hubbard's voice lifted into a shout, and others followed, stampeding the guards' loose horses out into the darkness.

Gunshots racketed and echoed. Shattuck shouted futilely, "Don't shoot! *I'm* here."

But firing continued. Some seemed to come from the town and some from the Hubbard rescue party, shooting back toward the flashes. Owen heard a sharp cry of pain. Tyson Hubbard shouted, "Vance!" Then everybody was spurring the horses into a hard run. Owen held to the saddlehorn to keep from falling. He felt his father's strong arm steadying him.

"Hang on, son. We got a ways to go."

Owen's head gradually cleared. He became able to sit up in the saddle. He was strong enough to grip with his legs and remain astride without help from Andrew. He could see the dark forms of horsemen on either side of him and knew there were seven or eight besides himself and Andrew. And Phineas Shattuck. Someone had bound Shattuck's hands to the saddle.

Owen looked behind him but saw no sign of the town. He judged that the horses had already run a mile or more. Somebody was slumped low in his saddle, two men on either side holding him on his horse.

Vance Hubbard had been hit.

Owen looked back again. Andrew said, "Ain't no use lookin'. They're back yonder someplace, after us."

Owen said bitterly, "I don't belong here."

"You don't belong dead, neither. They'd have you hangin' from a live oak limb by now."

"Maybe not. You didn't give me a chance to choose."

"Between livin' and dyin'? There *wasn't* no choice."

Someone declared grittily, "A boy ought not to talk back to his daddy." The voice belonged to Red Upjohn, the man who had talked about killing Owen in the thicket. He said sternly, "It's on account of you that Vance Hubbard has got a bullet in his back. I tried to tell him, but he said he owed you for the womenfolks."

Andrew Danforth declared, "Don't try to saddle my son down under that whole load. Vance did it for me, too." He pulled over near Hubbard for a better look at his condition. Tyson was holding his brother in the saddle. The look in his face said the situation was grave.

Andrew swore. "Shattuck, you've got a lot to answer for."

Shattuck stared at the ground moving beneath the feet of the horse upon which he was tied. Owen thought he heard a whimper.

Daylight came. Owen glanced back, expecting pursuit. He saw nothing, but he felt it was there. Shattuck turned too, and it seemed to Owen that the whites of his eyes showed large as he studied Vance Hubbard's slumped form. Tyson Hubbard looked at Shattuck, and the look promised death.

The morning sun was half an hour above the horizon when the riders passed over a hill and Owen saw the dense growth of the thicket ahead. No pursuit had shown itself. The horsemen slowed to a steady trot, then to a walk to make the pace easier for the wounded man. In the daylight, Vance Hubbard's face was gray as clabber and just as cold. The riders had stopped twice in the night to stanch the bleeding, but there had been neither time nor light to extract the bullet lodged in his back.

Now, in the edge of the heavy timber, time was taken. Though Owen still felt anger against his father for bringing this calamity upon them, he could no longer resent Vance Hubbard. Whatever Hubbard might have owed him, he had repaid, with interest.

Someone spread a thin blanket. Upjohn and another

man placed Hubbard upon it, on his stomach. Hubbard
bit his lip to suppress a cry, but a groan came anyway.
Tyson cursed the men for not being gentler with his
brother. Red Upjohn glared, and Owen felt he would
have knocked Tyson off of his feet had other consider-
ations not been more pressing. Andrew Danforth ripped
open the blood-soaked shirt and examined the swollen,
blue-edged wound. "Bullet's in there deep."

Tyson trembled, touching his brother. "We've got a
doctor in camp. A tooth-puller, is all, but he's got some
tools. If we try to cut on Vance here we may kill him."

Andrew worried, "He may not make it to camp."

Hubbard spoke painfully, "I can make it. Just put me
back on my horse and hold onto me. I'll get there."

Tyson pushed to his feet, his eyes blistering Phineas
Shattuck. "Here's *one* piece of excess weight we don't
need to be takin' no further. Banty, give me that rope
off of your saddle."

Banty was hesitant.

Shattuck cried, "No!" He looked around desperately
for help. "Please, I ain't done nothin' but my duty."

Tyson seethed, "And loved every minute of it. Banty,
your rope."

Banty just sat there, his mouth open in silent protest.
Someone else handed Tyson a coiled rope. He loosened
it.

Owen held his breath and waited vainly for someone
to stop this. Heart pounding, he looked to his father and
saw hesitation.

Shattuck began to weep. "Please, somebody . . ." His
gaze fastened hopefully on Owen. "Soldier, I wasn't really goin' to kill you. You ain't goin' to let them . . .
Please!"

Tyson shook out a loop and tossed it over Shattuck's

head. Shattuck tried desperately to dodge, but his movement was restricted by the thongs that bound his hands to the saddle. "No," Shattuck pleaded in a piping voice, "you can't do this." Tears spilled down his cheeks. "Please, I'm beggin' you . . ."

Owen saw in some of the men's faces that they were not strong for a killing. Upjohn surprised Owen by saying, "You don't really want to do this, Tyson. Hangin' is ugly. I seen my son . . ."

But no one actually moved to stop it. Owen listened to Shattuck's pleading and felt his stomach turn. Remembering Uncle Zach, he tried to tell himself it was justified. But he knew he could not let it happen. He stepped to Tyson's side and lifted a pistol from Tyson's waistband. He maneuvered quickly to put his back to the brush so no one could get behind him. He poked the weapon into Tyson's ribs.

"Take the rope off of him."

Tyson exploded in outrage, "Owen, you've wore out your welcome with me."

"I never asked for your welcome. I said take the rope off."

Andrew put in, "Son . . ."

Owen told him angrily, "You could've stopped it. You didn't."

"I wasn't sure I wanted to. I'm still not."

"*I* am. Dad, cut his hands loose." Tyson seemed about to pull away. Owen shoved the pistol into his ribs, hard enough to bruise. "Tyson, you stand real still."

To Owen's surprise it was Red Upjohn who came reluctantly to his support, not Andrew. Red declared, "The soldier boy's right for once, Tyson. Kill Shattuck thisaway and they'll call up half the troops in Texas to clear out the big thicket."

Using the saber he had once pointed at Owen's throat, he cut Shattuck's bonds.

A murmur rose among the men. Andrew Danforth looked around fearfully for any move against his son. "Everybody stand easy."

Shattuck, white-faced, slipped the loop from around his neck. He did not wait for a blessing. He drummed heels against the horse's ribs and tore away through the brush.

Owen stepped back from Tyson, but he held a firm grip on the pistol. "Don't anybody go after him."

Tyson's eyes brimmed with tears of anger. "You'll wish you hadn't done that."

"I'm already charged with treason for somethin' I didn't want to do. I won't have you pilin' murder on top of it."

Gravely Andrew said, "Just because you saved him, son, don't think Shattuck'll be forgivin' of you. It'll set hard with him that you saw him whine and beg for his life. If he ever gets you in his hands again there won't be any use in you beggin' *him*."

"He ain't goin' to get me in his hands."

Tyson's fury had not ebbed. "We ought to tie you out here at the edge of the brush and leave you for him to find. Then you'll see how much mercy he'll have."

Andrew stepped in front of Owen. "We don't need any more talk like that. There's your brother to see after."

Owen made a fist and defiantly moved out from behind his father. "I can take care of my own self."

From Vance Hubbard came a quiet pleading. "For God's sake, Tyson, take me to camp. Don't let me die here while you-all fight amongst yourselves."

Chapter 6

The faint smell of woodsmoke told Owen they were approaching the camp, though he saw but little through the heavy mixed timber, scrub and briars. He could not discern even a horse trail. The people who lived in this deep fastness took care not to repeat the same route in and out so much that the thick ground layer of fallen, rotted leaves would betray the way. Only an expert tracker could trail fugitives deeply into this dense sanctuary.

The men took turns helping young Tyson hold his brother in the saddle. Vance Hubbard seemed more dead than alive. They talked hopefully about his recovery once they brought him under the care of his womenfolk, but Owen had observed too many men wounded in military conflict. Not often had he seen a man look as used up as Vance Hubbard and survive. Regret weighed heavily upon Owen's shoulders.

The irony lay heavily on him, too, the fact that this had all started with his freeing of the Hubbard women so they could be with Vance and Tyson.

Damn this war, he thought with bitterness. *Who wanted it in the first place?*

How the men found the hidden camp was a mystery to Owen, but they drew into a clearing, part natural and part created by axes and muscle. Owen saw a dozen or more tents, some sizable, some only rough shelters rigged with sheets of stained canvas ranging from gray to yellow. Mrs. Hubbard bent over a campfire where a couple of smoke-blackened pots were suspended from an iron bar. She straightened to watch the riders enter the clearing. Her hands went to her throat as she recognized her oldest son slumped, a grim young Tyson holding him in his saddle. She called out and came running. Lucy Hubbard rushed from the largest of the tents, a bucket in her hand. She saw her brothers and dropped the bucket, dumping its water on the ground.

Owen held back out of the way. With his bad arm he would be little help in easing Vance down from the saddle. His father and Tyson Hubbard carried the wounded partisan into a tent. Mrs. Hubbard made one short cry, then gathered her wits and began to direct her son's handling.

A thin-faced little man hurried across the clearing with a small black bag. He would be the dentist Tyson had mentioned. Through the open front of the tent, Owen watched him probe the wound while Mrs. Hubbard held Vance's hands. Her lips were pinched almost white. Lucy knelt beside her brother and took up the blood with a piece of cloth so the dentist could work. Her face was drained pale, but she did not flinch from the task.

Vance lapsed into unconsciousness, or he might not have stood the pain. So far as Owen knew, he had not rallied enough to speak to Mrs. Hubbard or Lucy.

Bitterly Tyson Hubbard said, "I'd like to get my hands on the heel fly who done that to him."

Andrew said, "A price of war, son. Nobody wanted it."

"Somebody must've, or it wouldn't've happened." He looked around belligerently, giving vent to his frustration and anger. His gaze lighted on Owen. "If you hadn't stopped me, that Phineas Shattuck'd be dead now, like my brother's fixin' to be."

From inside the tent came Mary Hubbard's firm voice. "Don't be talkin' foolishness, Tyson. If you've got to blame somebody, blame *me* for wantin' out of that town. That's where it started."

Andrew placed his big hands on Tyson's shoulders. "Shattuck's got a lot to answer to the Lord for, but he didn't fire the shot that brought your brother down." He glanced at his son. "I know it helps when you can find somebody to blame for a thing like this, but nobody is, and *everybody* is. This war could've been stopped before it ever started if enough people had stood up and said their say. We let ourselves slide into it a little at a time till we couldn't climb up out of the hole anymore. In a way, we're all to blame for what's happened to your brother."

The men of the camp, including those who had participated with Hubbard in the Danforth rescue, stood around quietly, solemnly. They waited as Owen had so often seen soldiers do between battles, waiting for life, or for death, or for God knew what. It struck him that this clearing resembled a hundred military encampments he had seen at one time or another. Yet these were not soldiers so much as refugees. In that moment, though they represented a side against which he had fought and against which many of his friends had died, he felt pity for them in this austere exile.

A coldness came upon him as he considered that he had unwillingly become one of them. He did not know how he might ever return to his own side in this war. He looked to the heavy brush which seemed to press in against the rough clearing from all around. Even the wind could not properly move through the dense growth that surrounded him. He felt somehow choked, somehow imprisoned.

Red Upjohn moved up beside Owen as the operation continued in the tent. Owen saw an anger in the man that was hard to fathom. Upjohn growled, "If you'd never come home from the war, there wouldn't've been no need for us to raid the jail."

Owen had no wish to be drawn into a fight, but he could not let the remark pass unanswered. "If it hadn't been for some damnyankee's saber, I wouldn't've had to."

The little man named Jim Carew had seemed subservient to Upjohn before, but now he displayed an indignation that surprised Owen. "Red, this is a time to hold your silence. If you've got to exercise your mouth, go say a prayer for Vance."

Upjohn gave him a challenging stare, but Carew stood up to it. Upjohn backed away and went to see after his horse, which he had left tied with the saddle on.

Owen said quietly, "Thanks. I didn't want to fight him."

Carew gave Owen a look that said he was no happier with him than with Upjohn. "I almost had to fight him myself, after you run off from me yesterday. You left me in a tight place."

"I was in a tight place too. I told you I had to get home before Shattuck came lookin' for me. I didn't make it."

Carew nodded. "We followed you. We wanted to just ride in and pull you and your daddy out of that trouble a lot sooner, but Vance said surprisin' Shattuck at the jail wouldn't be as dangerous." He stared gravely toward the tent. "Even Vance Hubbard could be wrong."

Owen heard a metallic thump as the dentist dropped a lead ball into a tin pan. He heard the man telling Lucy to let the wound bleed and cleanse itself. "We seem to have more blood around here than medical supplies."

Mrs. Hubbard asked quietly, "What are his chances?"

The doctor was a moment in answering. He shook his head. "Ma'am, a lie would be a disservice to you."

Lucy reached quickly to grasp her mother's hand. Mrs. Hubbard did not look up. Andrew Danforth placed his hand on Mary Hubbard's arm, expressing with a touch what might not be said in words. Tyson Hubbard put his arms around his mother and his sister.

A raspy voice spoke, "Mama." Mrs. Hubbard bent over her son. "I'm here."

Owen had to strain to hear Hubbard say, "Mama, I wish . . ." The voice stopped there.

Mrs. Hubbard said, "I know. I know." She leaned her head down against him.

Vance asked, "Where's Andrew Danforth?

Andrew replied, "I'm with you, Vance."

"Andrew, watch out for my family. You and your boy, please see after them."

Andrew assured him, "We will." Andrew looked up at Owen, his eyes asking. Owen could only nod, wondering how he could help anyone else when right now he could hardly help himself. He found Lucy watching him through eyes that brimmed with tears. Probably wishing she could trade him for her brother, he thought.

He clenched his fist against a feeling half anger, half helplessness. If the two women had been content to remain in town, Vance Hubbard would not be dying. Owen would not be a fugitive from his own people, and most certainly he would not be a semicaptive here in the midst of this interminable thicket. But as he watched Mary and Lucy and Tyson Hubbard standing strong in their grief, he could hold no anger against them. This seemed not the time, not the place. There was blame enough, he thought, for everybody.

He wondered, as he had wondered many times on one dusty, red-spattered battlefield and another, how people so recently friends, Americans together, could have allowed such a madness to come about. He wondered if Andrew was right, that the people could have stopped it had they tried harder. Surely if they had known then what they knew now, they would have.

Vance Hubbard proved stronger than the camp had thought. He lived through the afternoon and most of the evening, seeming at times to drift away into unconsciousness but responding when spoken to. His family remained by his side. Andrew Danforth never strayed far, though once he came out to suggest that someone fix a meal for the women so they would not have to leave Vance. As darkness came and no one took it upon himself to post guards, Andrew called the men together and assumed that responsibility. Most of the men accepted without seeming to question the propriety or Andrew's right. Red Upjohn grumbled something about a newcomer taking over without even waiting for Hubbard to die, but he stopped when Carew angrily whispered an answer no one else could hear.

Andrew studied his son. "You willin' to stand your share of the duty?"

Owen made no effort to suppress his resentment. "What duty? If it was up to me, I wouldn't be here. If it hadn't been for you, I *wouldn't* be."

Red Upjohn declared, "You wouldn't put him on guard, would you, Danforth? He may be your son, but he's a Confederate. If any of his side was to show up, he'd join them against us."

Owen tried to think of a response. All that came was anger.

He heard Mary Hubbard's stern voice behind him. "Mr. Upjohn, Owen Danforth is here because he went beyond duty to help my daughter and me. None of us wants to be in this place, Owen least of all. But he *is* here and I'll expect you to make the best of it or leave my son's camp."

Taken by surprise, Upjohn touched his fingers to his hat brim. "I've got nothin' but respect for you, ma'am. I'm just thinkin' of the good of the camp and wonderin' if we can stand the risk of this soldier boy. His sympathies ain't changed."

"That makes him the most unfortunate of us all," she said firmly. She looked back toward the tent where Vance Hubbard lay. "Except for one."

"Yes ma'am," Upjohn said deferentially. But as he turned away his parting look told Owen he was simply being kind to an unfortunate woman. He had changed his mind about nothing.

Andrew Danforth shrugged. "All right, son. I *won't* put you on guard duty. You've got a bad arm anyway."

Owen snapped, "I watch with my eyes, not my arm.

Since you've gotten me into this mess, I'll stand my share of the duty. But Upjohn is right about one thing. If any of *my* people come along, I won't shoot at them."

Banty Tillotson grinned. It seemed to Owen that he grinned most of the time, whether there was anything to grin about or not. Banty said, "You don't need to worry, Owen. Anybody gets this far into the thicket by himself is lost anyway. He'll be beggin' you to shoot him."

Owen flexed the fingers of his left hand and found them less stiff than yesterday. He raised the arm gently until pain stopped him. Healing was slower than he would like, but it seemed to be coming. One of these days he would not have to let a woman take up his fight.

Andrew Danforth studied him worriedly. "I don't know what it'll take for Red Upjohn to have confidence in you."

Owen shook his head. "I don't give a damn. I just want him to leave me alone." He looked around the little camp, which in the dusk seemed even more hemmed in by the brush. "I wish *everybody* would leave me alone."

Andrew's eyes narrowed. "Me included?"

"You had the most to do with me bein' here. I've got a lot of things to sort out in my mind, and that's one of them. Another is what I'm goin' to do about it."

"I don't know what you *can* do about it. All the bridges seem to've been burned."

"With somebody else holdin' the torch."

Vance Hubbard clung to life until after dark. Owen heard a little cry from Mrs. Hubbard and knew the waiting was over. He saw the two women holding one another. Tyson stood with his arms around both. Owen removed his hat and stood slumped outside the tent. Even more than before, the camp seemed a cold and brooding place, sad beyond measure. He wanted to get away. But how? And where could he go?

It was impractical to herd the horses in the heavy brush, but a military-type picket line was not appropriate either. The grass was sparse, and keeping the horses so close together gave them little chance to graze. Instead, they were scattered, each staked on a long rope that gave it an opportunity to find sustenance, poor as it might be. To fetch hay or other feed into this thicket in any meaningful quantity was clearly out of the question.

Owen walked to the big bay, which stood at the end of a rope. The horse seemed already to have cropped off whatever grass might have been available to him. Or perhaps other horses had done it before. This was no place, Owen thought, for either men or horses to remain very long. He ran his hand along the heavy neck and down the shoulder. Temptation chewed at him. It would not be difficult, while everyone's attention was on the death of Vance Hubbard, to saddle the bay and ride out of here. But he had no personal knowledge of what lay beyond this brush except in the direction of town and home. In that direction, he could not go.

He felt in his shirt pocket for the paper which had given him permission to come home on convalescent leave. He was reassured to find it still there. It would have been easy to have lost it. He tingled to a sudden realization. Phineas Shattuck had scarcely looked at it. He probably had no idea to what military unit Owen belonged. It was unlikely the local courthouse had any record, either, for Owen had enlisted in San Antonio. If he could but get out of this place and escape capture until well beyond Shattuck's influence, the document should provide him safe passage through any checkpoints. He could rejoin his old outfit without anyone there knowing the trouble he had encountered at home.

A rough voice said, "You wasn't figurin' on leavin' us, was you?" He knew before he turned that the man was Red Upjohn.

Owen sagged in disappointment, for he had waited too long. "I suppose you'd put a bullet in my back if I was to try."

Upjohn grunted. "I'll bet if you offered to lead Shattuck and his guards to this camp, he'd drop all charges."

Owen could not deny the thought. But he had not permitted it serious consideration. "My dad's in here."

"Seems to me like everything ain't too pleasant between you and your daddy. Seems to me like you might even be mad enough to turn him in."

Owen demanded, "What kind of a Judas do you think I am?"

"How many kinds are there?"

The exchange had caught the attention of Tyson Hubbard. He came out and listened, then said evenly, "Owen, don't you get any notions about slippin' away tonight . . . or any other time. I'll be watchin' you."

Upjohn turned on Tyson with almost as much animosity as he had shown Owen. "You Hubbards brought him here. If it was up to me he'd already be dead."

Tyson flinched under the unexpected attack. "*You* can leave any time you take a notion, Red."

"And I will, if *I* decide to. Ain't nobody can tell me what to do. Especially no wet-eared kid too big for his britches." He stalked away like an angry old bull after a fight.

Banty Tillotson had followed Tyson. He managed an infectious smile that lifted a little of the tension. It seemed to Owen that Banty was the only perpetually good-humored man in this somber camp. "Don't you-all fret over what Red Upjohn says. Poor feller's got a rail or two missin' out of his fence."

Tyson grumbled, "We ought to run him out of this place. Seems like he's always startin' trouble in camp."

Banty said, "Ignore him. It ain't worth the worry."

Tyson jerked his head at Owen. "You come too. From now on, you stay away from the horses until one of us is with you."

Owen was not angry so much as disappointed over the idea that he had let an opportunity go by. But he realized Upjohn had probably been watching him all the time. Had Owen so much as reached for his saddle, he might have taken a bullet in his back. His gaze followed the bitter Upjohn, and he reflected that war's cruelties seemed to kill some people without making them stop breathing. Upjohn had been wounded deeply, in a place that showed only through the madness in his eyes.

Because the horses had eaten out all the grass within practical reach of the clearing, a decision was made to move camp a couple of miles to a place where a small seep would provide water enough for people and horses. Vance Hubbard was buried at the edge of the old camp, the place marked by a crude cross cut of hackberry limbs. That would have to serve until a better day, when something more appropriate could be done.

Lucy and Tyson Hubbard looked back as the small brigade put the clearing behind them and pushed into the brush, but Mary Hubbard forced herself to keep her gaze forward. Andrew Danforth rode beside her, a quiet sympathy in his eyes.

He had buried dreams of his own. Many of them.

Presently Andrew moved up to the front of the column, assuming by his nature a leadership that death had vacated. No one questioned the fitness of his doing so; the men seemed to accept. At one time or another he had helped many of them to reach the sanctuary of this great thicket. Despite his personal resentment, Owen could see in his father what he had seen in many officers he had served, a strength and confidence that others sensed without the requirement of noise or show.

Movement through the tangled brush was slow and tedious, the riders falling into several more or less parallel tracks, single file, ducking low branches, weaving a crooked pattern. Owen became aware, after a time, that he had lagged to the rear. A persistent notion came to him again. This might be his chance to pull away. By the time he was missed it would be too late for anyone to backtrack and find him.

A stern voice put an end to the notion. "I can read what's runnin' through your mind, Owen. I'd drop you before you could go twenty feet."

Tyson Hubbard had worked in behind him. And behind Tyson rode Red Upjohn. They had little use for one another, but Owen thought they had more in common than they realized.

He found to his surprise that he had unconsciously made a fist with his left hand. *That*, at least, was an improvement.

The brush thinned a bit. Lucy Hubbard slowed her horse until she fell back even with Owen. She turned in the saddle and glanced at her brother with challenge in her eyes. "Mind if I ride with Owen?"

He shook his head, figuring she would do what she wanted.

She said, "Me bein' here might help keep you out of trouble with my brother."

"I'm in no trouble with him."

"Looked like it to me. Are you so anxious to leave us?"

Owen was surprised that it showed so plainly. "I don't belong with this bunch. You know that. My dad knows it."

"What if he hadn't carried you out of that jail? You'd probably be dead now . . . like my brother." Her voice caught.

He let a little of his resentment return. "I doubt that'd make much difference to you."

"It'd make a lot of difference, Owen." She touched his hand. He started to pull it away but did not follow through. Her touch stirred him.

She said, "We owe you."

He glanced back toward her brother. "If you figure you owe me, talk to *him*. All I want is to get out of this place. I've got no interest in betrayin' anybody."

She nodded. "It wouldn't do any good right now, but give him some time to get over losin' Vance. And give *me* time too, Owen."

"Time for what?"

"I don't know yet. Just time." She went silent, looking toward the riders ahead. Owen stared at her, his blood oddly warm.

He could think of nothing which would make his position here more uncomfortable than to become involved with a Unionist woman. But the tingling sensation from her touch remained with him.

The site selected for the new camp was brushier than the other and required much ax work to clear places for the tents. Owen decided to try the growing strength of his left arm. He had been taking it from its crude sling and exercising it regularly, finding a little more flexibility from one day to the next. The hand still allowed only a weak grip, but at least he could hold an axhandle; the right hand and arm did most of the work. The first few times he swung the ax, the left arm protested with a stabbing of pain. He gritted his teeth and dared it to stop him. It did not.

His father watched him in silence. Owen paused to allow the weak arm to rest. He demanded, "Any advice?" His tone said he solicited none.

Andrew shook his head. "You'll do what you want to anyway. I'm glad to see the arm is better."

Owen spoke with gravel in his voice. "I just wish it hadn't waited so long. I wouldn't be here."

His father's eyes did not waver. "I don't know any more ways to say I'm sorry. I won't try again."

Owen gradually became aware that the group's isolation was less complete than it might seem. Always, men from camp were out scouting the thicket, watching for signs of intruders, patrolling the edges to help men who legitimately sought a way in, harassing and turning back any attempt by the authorities to penetrate this fastness. There were places where men like Banty Tillotson and Jim Carew and Red Upjohn sometimes rode to meet at night with collaborators on the outside, men who could tell what was happening in the rest of the world, who could advise them on the activities of Phineas Shattuck and his home guards. Andrew and Zach Danforth had performed that duty for a long time. Now Andrew was the successor to Vance Hubbard's leadership, and he depended upon others' eyes and ears.

This information seemed not to travel in just one direction, however. At times the reports indicated that the authorities were more aware of what was happening inside the thicket than they had any right to be. They seemed to know that Vance Hubbard was dead, which might be explained by Shattuck's having seen him shot. But they seemed also to know that Andrew Danforth had assumed the leadership, loose though it was. That might or might not have been just a good guess, Andrew said worriedly when Jim Carew brought him the report.

Owen perceived that his father began studying the men in camp more closely than before, and that the lines in his face seemed to darken with the passing days.

Upjohn's leaving always lifted the spirits of the men in the clearing, though their morale inevitably sagged again when he returned with his brooding eyes, his scowling ways. In contrast, Banty Tillotson's jaunty manner was a tonic to the somber encampment. It was a joy to see him riding in, that grin like sunshine through the trees.

Andrew's worry deepened when Red Upjohn came in a day overdue from a lone foray, taken on his own volition, into the open countryside. Upjohn made it no secret that he harbored reservations about Andrew's right to give orders in the camp, but he reported to him nevertheless. He said he had been discovered and almost caught by a heel fly patrol. He had taken refuge in the brush near the Danforth farm. The kid guards cautiously probed the edge of the timber but did not risk venturing far into it.

While he was there he had seen something else. Someone was working not only Andrew's farm but Zach's.

"Who?" Andrew demanded sharply.

Upjohn shrugged. "If I was to hazard a guess I'd say that Shattuck confiscated it for the government. And around here, he considers *hisself* to be the government."

Andrew reacted as if Upjohn had punched him in the stomach.

If Red Upjohn's news was disturbing, Carew's a couple of days later was worse. The man's horse was flagging badly as he pushed him into the little clearing. Banty Tillotson met him with a smile. "You look like you been on a two-day drunk, Jim, and your horse with you."

Andrew Danforth went to confer with Carew at the edge of camp, where he was unsaddling. Carew said, "I'm cold sober. You'll quit that silly grin too, Banty, when I tell you what I heard."

He had ventured all the way to town in the darkness to watch, to listen. His face was grim as he turned to the waiting Andrew.

"They're comin' to the thicket, Andrew. And this time it won't be just Shattuck and a few of them kid guards. This time he'll have two or three full companies of army troops. He's swearin' around town that he'll bring us in or kill us all."

Chapter 7

Sometimes Andrew Danforth reacted suddenly to news, and sometimes he took a while to chew on it. This time he chewed. He gave first Owen, then Carew a long, quiet contemplation. He turned to Banty Tillotson, who had walked up in time to hear.

"You've been out too. You hear anything like that?"

Banty's reaction was characteristically nonchalant. "Nope. Anyway, they've tried before. They ain't taken a man out of these thickets yet."

Carew said earnestly, "They've never tried it in the kind of force they're talkin' about." His manner showed he placed stock in what he had heard. "Always been a few kid guards or a bunch of bigmouths like Shattuck. Never been soldiers in strength ever tried an honest-to-God push through here."

Banty smiled condescendingly. "You're always lettin' your imagination run away with you, Jim. Sounds to me like Shattuck braggin', is all. I wouldn't lose no sleep over it."

Red Upjohn scowled at Owen. He said nothing, but Owen thought he read Upjohn's mind: *The trouble started when you came here.*

Mary Hubbard emerged from her tent, carrying a long-handled spoon. Andrew thoughtfully watched her stir a pot of beans suspended over a low-burning open fire. He turned his gaze to young Tyson Hubbard. Tyson seemed almost cheered by the news. Andrew asked, "What do you think your brother would've said?"

The young man's eyes were full of fight. "I don't know what he'd've said, but what *I* say is, let them come. We can rag them like a terrier. We'll hit them where they're not lookin' and scatter out through this brush like quail through tall grass. Not much risk they'd catch us."

"Not much," Andrew pondered. "But *some*."

Tyson declared, "I'm willin' to take my chances."

Andrew frowned. "Are you willin' for your mother and sister to take them with you?"

Tyson sobered. He looked at his mother. She stopped stirring the beans. Concern came into her eyes as she studied her son and Andrew.

Tyson asked, "What're you gettin' at, Andrew?"

"Even if we did what you're talkin' about, which I don't favor, there'd be too much danger here for the women."

Mrs. Hubbard did not suffer her curiosity to remain unsatisfied. She let the long spoon sink into the pot and walked up to the men, her arms folded. "I get a feelin' somethin' has come along which concerns me, Andrew."

Andrew looked to Carew, who told her what he had heard. Mary Hubbard's gaze fastened solemnly upon her son. She said, "I suspect, Tyson, that you want to go out there and fight them."

Stiffly he said, "We owe them that for Vance."

She replied firmly, "We owe it to Vance to stay alive until this war is over. That's what *he* was tryin' to do."

Andrew put in, "Mary, is there someplace you could go where Shattuck and his bunch wouldn't look for you? Kinfolks, maybe, that he wouldn't know about? Somebody not carryin' the name of Hubbard?"

"Over east, in Austin County . . . my brother, Ed Bradshaw and his wife Vi. Might be a problem to get there without somebody catchin' us, though."

Andrew's gaze lighted upon Owen. Owen was uncomfortable under the stern appraisal. Andrew said, "Son, you've been wantin' out of this thicket. How'd you like to take Lucy and her mother to their kinfolks?"

Owen's eyes narrowed. "That's how I got *into* this thicket."

"You haven't talked much since we've been here, but I know you've itched to get back to your outfit."

"I've wanted to get away from *here*," Owen admitted, glancing at the belligerent Red Upjohn.

"You still have your leave papers. They'd take you anywhere, once you got clear of Shattuck's country." His voice fell. "I'd hope you'd go someplace besides that damnable war. But I couldn't stop you the last time. This time I won't try."

Owen's pulse quickened at the thought of putting this thicket behind him. Even the battlefields seemed better, though he knew only time and distance made them so.

Tyson declared, "I don't like it. Owen's still a rebel. Come to a showdown, I'm not sure he'd pick my mother and sister over ol' Jeff Davis."

Andrew's eyes were unreadable. "He did once before.

That's how come he got in all this trouble. But you can watch him yourself, Tyson. You're goin' with them."

Tyson's mouth dropped open in protest, but Andrew raised his big hand. "Look at your mother, boy. She's lost one son. I know how she feels, because I've lost two. If you stayed here she'd keep lookin' back over her shoulder, worryin' about you. She might even turn back and fall into Shattuck's hands. You'll go for *her* good, not for yours."

Mary Hubbard gave Andrew a look that spoke of gratitude. Owen was startled by the thought that she might feel something more than simply gratitude.

Tyson shot a resentful glance at Owen. "I belong here, fightin' with the rest of you. That's what Vance would've done."

"We're not goin' to fight them," Andrew said. "We're goin' to evaporate in front of them like a dew in July. *That's* what your brother would've done."

Tyson stared at the ground. Andrew placed a hand on his shoulder. "There's more to it than just your mother needin' you. One of these days—pretty soon, likely—this war'll be over with. A lot of the people we're callin' enemy will be our friends again. You don't want to have to remember that you killed some of them. Best thing you can do is stay out of the fightin' till that time comes." He looked at Owen. "That would be the best for all of us."

Any reply would have courted argument. Owen made none. If he could not leave his father with good feelings, at least there was no point in leaving him with the internal scars of another fight between them.

Andrew forged ahead as if both Owen and Tyson had agreed, though neither actually had. He turned to Mary Hubbard and called Lucy from the tent. "You'll want to do your travelin' at night, at least till you're well past anyplace where people have heard of the Hubbards, or of Shattuck."

Relief was in Mrs. Hubbard's eyes. "I'll be glad to get Tyson away from here. Once we're with my family we'll keep him out of sight." Her voice turned worried. "I wish *you'd* go with us too, Andrew."

Andrew shook his head. "There'd be suspicion. I'd draw attention to you. Here I can at least slip out now and again and keep an eye on my farm."

A sadness came over her, mixed with a little of anger. "They've confiscated your farm, just like they've taken ours."

"For now," Andrew said evenly. "But when the war's over there'll be regular courts again, no matter how it turns out. Then we'll see who owns that farm, and yours."

Mary Hubbard suggested that a start be made as soon as possible, though the four might have to wait a time for darkness at the edge of the thicket before venturing into the open. She feared that the longer Tyson was given to study on the matter, the more argument he would raise. Once on the way, he would find it difficult to turn back. The noon meal finished, Red Upjohn watched as Owen threw his saddle on the big Yankee bay.

"I'd like to trade you out of that horse," he said. "He'd serve me well if the heel flies ever give me a run."

Owen replied, "I've got a long ways to travel before I get back to my outfit. It'll take this bay or somethin' as good to carry me there."

Owen's intentions had rankled Upjohn from the beginning. Owen considered that understandable in view of the man's politics, his story about being forced to watch the lynching death of a son. Upjohn turned to Tyson, who was saddling a horse for his mother. "You may not be the man your brother was, but it's a good thing you're goin' too, boy. Wouldn't surprise me none if this one was to turn your womenfolks in. He'd like to get himself pardoned for helpin' them the first time."

Tyson gave Upjohn a startled glance. He was used to nothing except abuse from the man. He turned a hard stare on Owen. "He might *think* about it. But he'd find himself shakin' hands with the devil quicker'n a dog can swaller a biscuit."

Owen choked down a surge of animosity. It was useless to argue. Upjohn was a bitter, driven victim of the war, and Tyson was a hotheaded young fool trying to be a man but not knowing how. Owen was determined to make allowances, no matter how difficult. Lucy helped by walking up and standing quietly beside him. He asked which horse she wanted. She pointed to a black, which Owen considered a sound choice for traveling the night in secret.

She remained close beside him as he put the blanket and the saddle on her horse. He said, "Lucy, I've got no intention of lettin' the heel flies catch you."

"I know that."

"I wish you'd tell your brother. The suspicions he's got, he's liable to shoot me if I even sneeze."

"He'll be better when we get him away from this place." She held the black horse's reins while Owen cinched up. "I'm glad *you're* goin' with us. I've felt guilty for what me and Mama did to you. We played on your sympathy, you know. We knew what we were doin'."

"I never had any doubt of that."

"You could've ridden off and left us any time." She reconsidered. "No, I guess you couldn't. That's where we had you. But maybe you *should* have."

"Could be. Just don't give me any trouble this time."

She told him earnestly, "I'll never do anything like that to you again. I wouldn't have before if I'd known you." She touched his hand, and the touch was warm. "I know you now."

Owen turned away, wondering uneasily if he knew *her*.

He realized he should have told his father good-bye in a proper manner, but they had only stared at one another. The ghosts of two dead young Danforths stood between them, even at parting.

As Owen expected in view of the early start, they reached the eastern edge of the thicket while the sun was still two hours high. Owen and Tyson dismounted and led their horses cautiously to the fringe, studying the rolling, mostly open country beyond.

Tyson said impatiently, "I don't see nobody out there. We could sure use the daylight for travelin'."

"So can the heel flies. For all we know, there could be twenty of them just over that rise."

"Or there might not be any for twenty miles. I feel like a coward brushin' up this way, waitin' for dark so we can go sneakin' out."

"Your brother must've spent a lot of time brushed up, waitin'. I never heard anybody call *him* a coward."

Tyson said no more about his impatience, though he continued flexing his hands nervously.

Tyson's dun horse had a temperament to match his rider's. Baring its teeth, it stretched its neck and attempted to take a bite out of the big bay horse's hide. The bay squealed and whipped around to defend itself, almost jerking the reins from Owen's hand.

Owen asked irritably, "Is that the best horse you could pick?"

"Nothin' wrong with him. He's a good judge of character."

Owen pulled aside to keep the bay out of the dun's reach. "We ought to rest awhile. We'll likely ride all night."

"I ain't rested since the night Vance was shot."

"Then at least quiet down so your mother and sister can." Owen was surprised by the command he put into his voice.

Tyson said resentfully, "Now you're givin' orders like your daddy. But at least he's on *our* side."

"I'm on the side of not gettin' caught. You stay here if it suits you. I'm goin' to tell the women they'd ought to rest. And I figure on doin' the same."

He left Tyson by himself. In a little while Tyson came to where the others' horses were tied. The women lay on blankets. Owen had stretched out on the ground beneath a big hackberry tree. He opened his eyes just enough to see Tyson without betraying that he was watching. Tyson looked around irritably, as if tempted to voice his objections, then seated himself near his mother. He did not lie down. He took out a pocketknife and began whittling on a long stick, taking out his frustrations with the blade. By dusk the stick had been reduced to a toothpick, and he was surrounded by a pile of curled shavings.

Owen pushed to a sitting position and said, "It'll be dark pretty soon. I favor us eatin' a bite."

They ate jerky and cold bread brought from the camp. *Poor fixings*, Owen thought, but he had done worse many a time, back where the real war was. They saddled. Figuring Tyson would disapprove of any choice he made, he said, "One of us had better ride out in front and the other stay close by the women. Which'd you rather do?"

Tyson made no secret of his distrust. "Reckon I'll scout. Anyhow, I know the way to our kinfolks'."

"Suit yourself," Owen said, knowing he would in any event.

They skirted the edge of the brush at first because the thicket continued a couple of miles more, parallel to their intended direction of travel. That would allow them a quick retreat back into cover. But soon the thicket fell behind them, and only an occasional dark motte of timber offered shelter. Should they encounter travelers on the open road they could only pull off out of the way, dismount and hope darkness would prevent their being noticed. For a time nervousness goaded Owen like a sharp spur. Every bird which trilled in the distance sounded like the jingle of a curb chain or a spur rowel. He could not sustain that level of agitation indefinitely, however. Eventually he eased.

"You-all doin' all right?" he asked the women, trying to force confidence into his voice.

Lucy replied, "We're well protected. What do we have to be worried about?"

Owen wished he shared her faith.

He watched the stars for time and direction. He judged they had ridden a couple of hours when Tyson turned the dun back in a long trot from his position fifty yards forward. "I hear somebody comin' down the road," he whispered urgently.

There was no motte, but a short way out from the wagon ruts stood a stone fence upon which some settler had invested years of hard labor in off times when he could spare the hours away from his plow. The fence stood about chest high and looked black against the sliver of pale moon.

Owen said, "Let's get over against that. If we stay low, maybe they won't see us."

The women moved quickly, and Tyson followed. The four dismounted and crouched. The horses' heads would show above the fence, and in Owen's agitated imagination the dun color of Tyson's mount seemed to glow in the dark. Owen hoped whoever was coming would regard the horses as loose stock and pay no particular attention.

He listened to the hoofbeats, still at some distance. He heard a low murmur of conversation, a sloshing sound as if one of the horses had drunk too much water. He held his hand over his bay horse's nose to prevent its nickering a welcome to the others. His mouth turned dry as old leather.

Tyson muttered. His mother shushed him.

Owen thought, *I'm glad you weren't in any army outfit with me. You might've gotten us killed.*

There were two riders. One sang in a rough, off-key voice, stopping only to tilt his head back. A bottle caught the moonlight and reflected a silvery light. Owen heard the other rider say, "I want a little more of that before you finish it all." The voice was middle-aged, or older. The horses looked to be long in the tooth too, from what Owen could tell by their shapes and tired manner of movement.

Farmers, he decided with relief. They had not even noticed the four horses against the stone fence.

When the travelers were safely past, Tyson said with some resentment, "Just a couple of old codgers. Look at the time we've wasted. We could've just ridden on by them and they wouldn't've paid us no mind."

Owen said, "But if somebody stopped them farther down the road and asked them, they'd remember they saw us."

Tyson said, "I'm lookin' forward to the day when we can ride up and down these roads without havin' to hide. When the Union wins the war . . ."

Owen interrupted him testily. "You fixin' to lead the way, or do you want me to?"

Tyson's dun took a parting bite at Owen's bay. Tyson seemed to take pleasure in that.

They came across no one else that night, though they suffered a few anxious minutes when Tyson spotted something on the road ahead and feared it might be a patrol. Half a dozen cows were bedded down for the night in the broad ruts worn by hoofs and wagon wheels. The sleepy cattle pushed up hind end first and moved warily aside for the horses. A calf trotted off in fright, then bawled for its mother.

As dawn began to bring light in the east, Tyson pulled out of the trail and pointed to a heavy stand of timber perhaps a quarter mile from the trail. He disappeared around a hill while Owen accompanied Mary and Lucy Hubbard toward the trees. Tyson reappeared, pushing his horse into an easy trot. He caught up at the edge of the timber.

"Farmhouse on the yonder side of the hill," he said. "Wasn't nothin' comin'. We could make a little more distance if you-all feel like riskin' it."

Owen said, "No use pushin' our luck."

"I just want to get back where I belong," Tyson declared to his mother. "And that don't mean hidin' out with kinfolks."

She seemed disposed to meet his challenge, but she was startled by a loud snorting and a clatter in the timber. Owen reached for the pistol in his belt, stopping when he saw three half-wild hogs that had wandered upon the riders unexpectedly and had whipped back to escape. It was common practice for settlers to turn hogs loose in the timber to fatten on acorns. They became so wild, sometimes, that the grown ones could be brought down only with bullets. The easier-caught shoats made good eating, cured and left their appointed time in the smokehouse.

"Damn!" Tyson exclaimed. "I thought the heel flies had us. That spotted one looked kind of like Phineas Shattuck."

Mary Hubbard reproached her son. "That kind of language is not necessary in front of your sister."

Lucy smiled. "Let him be. I've heard a lot worse. Even said worse myself." She turned the smile on Owen. "That shock you?"

Owen shook his head. "I've always had my suspicions." He pointed his chin. "We ought to go a little deeper into these woods before we make camp. I'm thinkin' there's apt to be a creek in there somewhere. Me and Tyson can take turns sittin' out here on watch."

Tyson said, "If we could catch us a shoat, it sure would beat the cold bread and jerky and stuff we brought with us."

Owen reminded him, "Shattuck's the one that used to be a pig thief. I don't care to join his class."

The women were tired, and Tyson looked worse. After they had eaten the little that passed for breakfast, Owen said, "You-all get some rest. I'll watch."

For once Tyson offered no argument. He unrolled a blanket beside the little stream they had found, doubled it and flopped down as if he had been knocked in the head by an axhandle. Lucy gave her brother a look of compassion but said, "Don't you take the whole day on yourself, Owen."

Owen warmed at her show of concern. "I'll be all right."

He judged it was near noon when he saw a movement far back along the road. Six horsemen rode at a trot, spurring into an easy lope for a time, then dropping back to the slower pace, sparing their horses. They had just enough amateurish military manner to make him suspect they were heel flies. His mouth went dry again. He half expected them to turn off and investigate the timber. They remained on the road, passing over the hill, disappearing in the direction of the farmhouse Tyson had told about.

Owen's pulse slowed to normal. But the horsemen were still riding through his mind when a noise made him turn quickly, hand dropping to the pistol.

Lucy Hubbard said, "Don't you shoot me, Owen Danforth, or I may never speak to you again."

"What're you doin' here? You're supposed to be restin'."

"Tyson's still asleep. I thought I'd come and spell you awhile . . . let *you* rest."

"You're a woman. I couldn't let you stand watch."

"Why not? My eyes are as good as yours, I expect. If I saw somebody comin' I'd wake you up. That's all *you'd* do, isn't it, wake us up to travel in a hurry? You sure don't figure on havin' a fight with anybody."

"I don't figure on havin' one with *you*. Guard duty is a man's job."

"Well, I'm here. You can either go back to camp and rest or you can lie down where you're at."

"I couldn't sleep with you here."

She smiled thinly. "I'm not askin' you to sleep with

me. That'll come later, if I decide to marry you."

He felt as if nettles burned his face. "I'm tryin' to be serious with you, Lucy."

"So am I, Owen. When this war is over, I may want to be *real* serious."

She showed no sign of leaving, and any sleepiness he might have felt had abandoned him. She seated herself on the ground beside him. The closeness aroused him in a way he found unnerving. On the one hand he wanted to get up and leave, quickly. On the other he fought a strong wanting which said to reach out and take her, to throw himself upon her. He sensed that she knew his conflicting emotions and that she intended him to feel them. He wanted her here, yet he resented her manipulation.

She touched his hand. "I didn't mean to upset you, Owen. I'll go if it'll make you feel better."

She started to push herself up from the ground. He caught her wrist and pulled her back. "No. Stay."

She looked at him, smiling, and kissed him.

A faint smell of woodsmoke drifted to him from back in the timber. He told Lucy, "You better go warn them not to let that fire get any size to it. It's liable to draw visitors."

Lucy said, "They know that," but she went anyway. In a while she was back with a cup of coffee. "Mama said she stood it as long as she could. Here, this'll give you strength."

"I've *got* strength. What I need is to be out of this trap and back to where I don't have to worry about anything except Yankee soldiers." He accepted the cup, however, blew across it a few times, took a long swallow and sighed. "You can tell your mother she sure knows how to make coffee."

"So do I," Lucy responded. "You'll find that I'm a pretty good cook myself. I'll show you someday, when we're all back where we belong."

He frowned. "You ever goin' to quit raggin' me?"

"Someday, when I've got you."

"Some Yankee soldier or some heel fly may get me first."

"You won't let that happen. It wouldn't be fair to *me*."

Tyson Hubbard came out eventually, carrying his rifle at arm's length. He looked suspiciously at his sister. "It take two of you to watch?"

Lucy replied, "Owen watches the road. I just watch Owen."

"Don't you be forgettin' that he's still a Reb soldier. It was his kind that killed our brother."

Owen said tightly, "Those people aren't soldiers. They're not even a good imitation."

"They're good enough to kill somebody." Tyson went rigid, staring toward the road. He brought up the rifle, cradling it. Owen turned. From around the hill came a man riding bareback on a heavy-boned old plow horse, plodding deliberately toward the timber. Tyson leveled the rifle.

Owen raised his hand. "Wait. He don't look to me like a heel fly, much less a soldier."

"I ain't fixin' to shoot him, unless he gives me cause." But anxiety in Tyson's face showed he would need little cause.

Owen motioned Tyson and Lucy back into the timber. "It's probably the man who owns the place. Maybe he's huntin' his hogs."

"And maybe he's spyin' for the government," Tyson said, walking backward, unwilling to turn away from the oncoming stranger.

They retreated farther back into the woods. The rider stopped, finally. "Howdy in there!" he shouted. "You folks in yonder, I'm fixin' to come in. Don't you-all shoot me."

Owen gave Tyson a quick glance to see that the rifle was not aimed at the figure he could see vaguely through the foliage. "He knows we're here. We'd just as well talk. Lucy, you go back yonder with your mother."

She made no argument, turning and walking briskly through the trees. Tyson said, "If he makes one wrong move . . ."

Owen called, "Come on in, mister, but keep your hands where we can see them."

The farmer pushed the big horse a little way into the timber, his hands at chest level. "I got no weapon on me," he said evenly. "I ain't come to make trouble. I come to give you warnin'."

Owen walked cautiously around the farmer and his horse, looking for a firearm and seeing none. The man was large and muscular. He reminded Owen of his father and Uncle Zach. Every deep line in that craggy face had probably been graven honestly by the hard work and constant worry that is forever the farmer's lot. The big hand the man extended in friendship bore the calluses and scars of ax and hoe and plow. Owen accepted the hand and winced under its crushing grip.

Tyson took the hand with reluctance, and then backed off in distrust.

The man said, "I'm Heck Frazier. My place is around the hill yonder. This is my timber you-all are takin' your rest in, and welcome to it, I might say. My milk cow got out last night. I was lookin' for her about daylight when I seen you folks turn off of the road and come up here."

Owen felt foolish. "You saw us?"

"You-all ain't too experienced at the outlaw business, I reckon. I would've just figured you were soldiers takin' French leave if I hadn't seen the womenfolks with you. There's been more'n a few stopped in this thicket to catch their breath. Then, when them heel flies come by the house and asked if I'd seen two men and two women . . ."

Owen swallowed. "You didn't tell them?"

"I'm sixty-two years old, sonny, and I didn't get there by pokin' my nose in where it wasn't wanted. I just told them I'd been workin' all day and wouldn't've seen a train of elephants if they had happened to pass by." He gave Owen and Tyson each a moment's study. "One of you'd be Hubbard, I reckon, and the other one Danberry."

"Dan*forth*."

"Them heel flies know you-all by name. Asked me if I know anything about a family by the name of Bradbury or Bradshaw or somethin' like that over in Austin County."

Tyson cursed softly. "That's Uncle Ed. We was goin' to his place."

The farmer shook his head. "If I was you, I wouldn't. They seemed to know an awful lot about your plans."

Tyson's eyes were angry. "How could they? Unless they caught somebody from the camp and made him tell."

Owen felt his stomach churn. "Or maybe they didn't have to. Maybe they've had a man of their own in there all along."

"A spy? But I know them all," Tyson protested. "There ain't a one of them . . ." His face clouded as he reluctantly accepted the reality. "If I ever find out who he is . . ."

Owen turned back to the farmer. "We're much obliged, Mr. Frazier. Only thing I wonder is, how come you told us?"

Frazier shrugged. "I don't care for them heel flies. Don't mistake me: I got two boys in the Texas army. I mean, I *had* two. Lost one of them the first year of the war. Other one I ain't heard from in a long time. Don't have no idea where he's at." Sadness was in his eyes. "We was all Americans once. I pray God for the day when we'll all be Americans again." He cleared his throat. "You-all probably need fresh meat. If one of my shoats comes to hand, feel welcome. I'll bid you God's blessin', and good day." He remounted and rode back out of the timber.

Owen turned to Tyson. "Your mother and sister have to go somewhere else now."

Tyson agreed, but Mary Hubbard did not. Her jaw set hard as Owen and Tyson repeated the farmer's story. She declared, "We're goin' on to Ed's and Vi's."

Owen argued, "But the heel flies'll be there."

"You think I could leave this country without knowin' if they did somethin' to my brother and his wife?" She shook her head stubbornly. "You can leave us if you want to, Owen, but us Hubbards'll see about our kin."

Owen looked at Lucy and shrugged. They were his kin too, almost. "I'm come this far," he said. "I'll stay with you."

Chapter 8

It had always seemed to Owen during his military experience that the worst predicaments came from his company's being led into a situation for which officers had no proper plan but up and went anyway. That seemed the situation now. He had pondered for hours on the way and had come up with no idea that did not offer more hazard than promise.

From the brushy knoll where he stood in darkness with Tyson and Mary and Lucy Hubbard, the Bradshaw house three hundred yards down the slope was vague in shape, menacing in its blackness beneath a smothering dark canopy of large trees. In the quarter hour or so they had watched, they had seen no lamp or lantern. There had to be a sentry, perhaps more than one. Owen had seen horses standing loose in a corral—too many, Mary Hubbard said, for her brother to own. They must belong to the heel flies.

Her voice was tense. "If they've hurt Ed or Vi . . ."

Tyson said, "The only way we'll know is for me to go down there and have a look."

Owen had always admired nerve, but he deplored rashness. "How do you figure to see without *bein'* seen?"

Tyson pointed. "There's a strip of brush yonder that stretches almost to the barn. I can use it for cover."

"I doubt they've got your aunt and uncle in the barn. They'd be in the house. And whatever heel flies aren't out on guard are probably in there with them."

"Once I get to the barn I ought to be able to spot any lookouts they got and work around them. I can sneak like a wolf when I've got to."

"Sounds to me like the wolf is fixin' to sneak into the trap. They'll swallow you up."

Logic was no deterrent to Tyson. "I'll figure that out when I get there."

Owen had known Tyson's kind in the war, supremely confident in their ability to do anything imagination might invent. He had seen a few win medals. He had seen more of them buried with honors. He said as much.

Tyson demanded, "You got any better notion?"

Owen admitted he did not. "Maybe I'll get one while I go down there with you."

Mary Hubbard said, "I don't want you boys takin' chances."

Owen resisted the temptation to declare that he had already taken the biggest chance, agreeing to fetch them here. "I can't promise you anything, Mrs. Hubbard, except that we'll try. If we don't come back in an hour or so, you and Lucy better be puttin' some miles behind you before daylight. Go to some kin that the heel flies wouldn't know about."

Lucy caught Owen's hand and held it fearfully. Mrs.

Hubbard said, "We won't talk about such as that. You boys are comin' back."

Owen grunted some kind of answer and mounted his horse. He and Tyson rode cautiously, ducking the low, raking limbs as they worked their way through the long strip of brush. For all of her expressed concern, Owen knew Mary Hubbard had left them no alternative. They had to go down to the house for a look. He wished for all of Tyson's confidence and twice his common sense.

That family was a single-minded lot, he thought, from the late Vance Hubbard to his mother and Tyson. Lucy was probably just as hardheaded. He wondered if he had implied any commitment to her that he might come to regret.

He followed because Tyson knew the place and the way. An old, too-familiar dread built in Owen's stomach, as it always had before any fight he had known was coming. He had never understood people who showed none of it or claimed they never felt it. He had always regarded them as fools or liars.

Tyson dismounted within the cover of the brush. He did not look back, taking it for granted that Owen would follow his lead without question. Owen *had* questions, but he held them.

Tyson pointed and whispered one word, "Barn."

I can see that for myself, Owen thought with a quick irritation. The barn was a swayed log structure twenty or thirty yards beyond the fringe of scrub timber. Beyond that extended the aging corrals, and beyond the corrals the log house with its traditional two sections under one roof, an open dog run between. Owen judged it to be fifty or sixty yards away. It might as well be fifty miles for all the chance he could see of reaching it undiscovered, unless all the heel flies had forsaken their duty and gone to sleep. That was a possibility if no mature and responsible man had come with them on this mission to impose discipline.

Tyson whispered, "Let's make a run for the barn."

Owen grabbed his arm firmly enough to give pain. "Let's not. Let's watch awhile."

Tyson wrested his arm free. He was about to go anyway when something moved beside the barn. Owen caught Tyson's arm again. Tension had brought Tyson's muscles to steel hardness.

The figure seemed no more than a shadow at first, slowly taking form as Owen concentrated on it. Moving out of the pool of darkness beside the barn, it took on the shape of a man walking slowly and without evident purpose, loosely carrying a rifle at arm's length. The guard rounded the corner, took a long and uneasy look toward the house, then lowered himself to the ground and rested his back against the barn's tough wall.

Not much of a sentry, Owen thought. Probably one of those half-grown buttons of the type Phineas Shattuck liked to boss around. Away from Shattuck or other authority, it was natural for boys of that self-asserting age to do as they pleased. It pleased this one to rest.

Tyson whispered, "If he nods off to sleep, we can sneak up and hit him on the head."

"He's just a kid. I don't want us hurtin' him if we don't have to."

"He's a damned Confederate."

Owen bristled. "So am I. I'm here to help your womenfolk, and that's all. I didn't come to hurt my own people."

"Heel flies ain't people."

"They're just kids, most of them. Whatever quarrel

we've got is against people like Shattuck. They tell them what to do."

The sentry sat with arms folded across his knees, head against his arms. Presently the rifle slipped from his fingers and slid slowly down the boot tops that covered his shins. It came to rest across one foot. The boy did not move.

"He's gone," Tyson said.

He was not, altogether. Tyson's dun horse chose that time to bare his teeth and take a bite at Owen's big bay. He was tied too far to reach him, but the squeal of equine anger brought the sentry's head up. He reached down for the rifle and looked around in confusion. Tyson moved to quiet the horse, but the boy was already aroused. He pushed warily to his feet, the rifle up and ready. Owen realized the boy did not know from what direction the sound had come. He seemed, after a minute, to conclude that it had been made by the horses in the corral. He walked to the fence, grumbling at the animals to quit making a fuss. He succeeded only in stirring them up.

When no other sentries appeared, Owen whispered, "That must be the only lookout they've got." It stood to reason. Boys sent on a man's errand remained boys.

Tyson said, "Now's our chance to make it to the barn."

Owen had no clear idea what advantage that might yield them, but Tyson was not burdened by Owen's doubts. He sprinted from the brush to the heavy shadow of the barn. Owen took one more look to be sure the sentry had not seen, then followed him, talking under his breath about what happened to people who leaped first and looked afterward. He flattened himself against the barn.

The sentry came slouching back, rifle again at arm's length. He was looking over his shoulder, muttering about fool horses. He almost bumped against Tyson.

Tyson touched the cold muzzle of a pistol against the young man's throat. He whispered, "I'd be obliged if you'd give me that rifle, real careful and quiet."

Astonished, the young man simply turned loose. The rifle fell to the ground with a light clatter. Eyes wide as dollars, the guard raised his hands. Owen stooped to pick up the weapon and took a good look at the face. "I know you. Name's Adcock, isn't it?"

This was one of the boys Owen had caused to drink himself into a stupor on the Hubbards' porch, a boy he had seen Shattuck chastise unmercifully afterward. Adcock moaned, "You're that soldier Danforth. You've done it to me again. Shattuck'll have me shot."

Tyson threatened, "Make any wrong move and we'll do it for him. We want to talk to you a little bit." He motioned toward the brush. "Let's go out there where nobody's apt to come up on us unawares."

The boy lamented, "Oh Lordy, he just won't understand this at all. He'll have me court-martialed and shot." But he went as Tyson indicated with a motion of his pistol barrel. Adcock looked apprehensively back over his shoulder.

When they reached the brush Owen turned to survey the barn and house. He half expected to see other sentries come running, but even the horses had gone quiet in the corral.

Tyson kept the pistol under young Adcock's chin. "Now, what've you-all done to the people who live in that house?"

"We ain't done nothin' to them," Adcock protested. "Johnson, he's in charge. He just told them not to go outside or nothin'. Said there wouldn't nothin' happen to them if they followed orders." He stared fearfully at Tyson or at Tyson's pistol. "They *are* your kinfolks, ain't they?"

"What did they tell you?"

"Said their names was Bradshaw and they didn't have no kin by the name of Hubbard. We'd about decided the informer was mistaken."

Owen demanded, "What informer?"

Adcock stiffened. "I done said too much. I ain't tellin' you anymore."

Tyson angrily grabbed Adcock's shirt and jerked him against the muzzle of the pistol. "By God you will!"

Owen caught Tyson's arm. "Hold off. Don't hurt him. I think we ought to be able to make a trade, us and him." Tyson eased back, releasing his hold. Adcock whimpered, plainly afraid he was breathing his last. Owen felt sympathy, remembering his own vulnerability at that age.

Owen tried to make his voice reassuring. "We can help each other, boy. You've got a choice. We can leave you tied up, and they'll know we caught you. You already said Shattuck's liable to shoot you. Or we can leave you to go back to your post without anybody ever knowin'. The only way they'd find out would be if you told them yourself."

Adcock glanced hopefully from one captor to the other. "You'd do that, and not get me in more trouble than I already am?"

Owen nodded and looked as honest as he knew how. "You just tell us the truth. Nobody ever needs to know you went to sleep on the job."

"Tellin' you anything would be like treason."

Owen shook his head. "Not when you can't help it.

You're in a trap, same way I was. All we want is to keep Shattuck from catchin' our people. We're a thousand miles from the fightin', and what happens here won't make any difference to the real war."

Tyson pressed, "Who told Shattuck we figured to come to this place?"

Adcock shrugged. "All I know is that Shattuck's had somebody in the thickets with you people for a good while now, slippin' him information about who's in there, and what you-all're up to."

Tyson cursed. "If you don't know his name, tell me what he looks like."

"I can't. I ain't never seen him that I know of. That was officer doin's. They never told me none of that stuff."

Tyson caught Adcock's shirt again. Owen pulled Tyson's wrist away. He was surprised, suddenly, to realize he had used his left hand. The wounded arm had gained more strength than he had realized. "No use hurtin' him." He turned to Adcock. "We heard Shattuck intends to invade the thicket in force."

Adcock nodded. "He's got a bunch of regular soldiers on the way. Time comes, that spy'll slip out of you-all's camp and lead them in there. Shattuck figures them he can't capture, he'll kill. Them he captures, he'll hang."

The dread came again, stronger than Owen had ever felt it. His stomach seemed weighted, cold as December. "Dad wouldn't figure on that, somebody guidin' the soldiers in."

Tyson Hubbard grimaced. "Vance wouldn't've either. He always figured his protection was the Confederates not knowin' their way through the thickets." He stared bitterly at Adcock. "For all we know, this'n could be the one shot him that night as we were ridin' away from town."

Adcock cringed from the threat in Tyson's eyes. "It wasn't me. I never drawed a gun." Desperately Adcock told more than he had been asked. "It wasn't none of us that shot your brother. It was the informer done it. He taken advantage of the confusion and all the shootin'. He got behind Vance Hubbard and put him out of the way."

Tyson swore. "I'm goin' back there, Owen. I'll find out who he is and kill him!"

"We may not go anywhere if we rouse up the rest of Adcock's bunch. Settle down." He gazed sternly at Adcock. "Anything else you can tell us about that spy?"

Adcock held his fearful gaze on Tyson Hubbard. "I already told you more than I know."

Owen unloaded the youth's rifle and handed it to him. "You go back to your post. Act like nothin' happened, and Shattuck won't ever know the difference. If you don't peach on us, we won't ever have to peach on you."

Adcock walked hurriedly across the open space to the barn. It obviously took a strong effort on his part not to run.

Tyson said between clenched teeth, "I never seen a heel fly I could trust."

"You can trust his fear. He's scared to death of Shattuck." Owen moved toward the horses. "Let's get back to the women."

Owen recounted to them briefly what he and Tyson had learned. "I feel like Adcock told us the truth; they haven't hurt your kinfolks at the house. When we don't show up here the boys'll finally decide the whole thing was a mistake and go home. Adcock sure won't tell them any different. And while they're waitin' here you-all can be ridin' on to other kin that Shattuck doesn't know about."

Mary Hubbard frowned. "Owen, are you still figurin' on goin' back to your army?"

Owen nodded. "That's been my intention all along."

Her eyes were more severe than he had ever seen them. "I know you and your father have had your disagreements. But he's a good man. That boy put a whole new complexion on everything. If you ride away from here now, Owen, you're not the man I thought you were. Your father and the others . . . they've got to be warned."

Owen's eyes met Tyson's. "They will be. Me and Tyson are both goin'. I don't know the thicket well enough to find the way by myself."

Tyson argued, "Ain't no use in that. You see Mama and Lucy to where they're goin', then head on back to your damned army. I can tell your dad about the informer."

"You can't tell him everything I need to. There's been a wall between me and him. After this, we may never see each other again. I don't want to remember that we parted in a strain."

There was more, a fear that Tyson would do something rash and never reach the men in the thicket. But he saw no use in speaking that concern and rousing Tyson's indignation.

Lucy leaned to Owen, her arms spread for him. She said, "Don't you worry about Mama and me. You just watch out for yourself and Tyson. When this is over with . . ."

Owen kissed her. "I'll come huntin' you."

"I'll be easy to find."

Tyson stared incredulously at the couple, then looked to his mother for an explanation. She did not attempt one. Mary Hubbard hugged her son and beseeched him not to let himself come into harm's way. Then she and Lucy were riding eastward, and Owen and Tyson spurred west. In a moment, looking back, Owen was unable to see the women. A sense of loss settled darkly over him, and it stayed a long time.

He and Tyson rode faster going back, taking risks. They traveled by day as well as by night, though they avoided the main trails where traffic would have increased the hazard of discovery. At one point they dismounted behind a tall stone fence and watched a troop of cavalry moving on the road. Except for the officer who rode in front, the men had no military uniforms. The Confederacy lacked the resources to clothe its army in style; this late in the war it did well to furnish weapons.

Tyson said, "Reckon they're on their way to join Shattuck's invasion?"

Owen shrugged. "Might be." He felt a little of anger. "Seems like with the fightin' to be done against the Yankees, they oughtn't to waste all this effort on a harmless little bunch of dissidents hidin' out in the brush."

"Dissidents hell! We're patriots. You damned Rebs are the dissidents."

It was an old argument fought too many times and never won. Owen said, "Come on, let's go." He climbed back upon the bay and spurred off, letting Tyson labor to catch him.

As he rode, he reviewed in his mind all the men he had met in the thicket. That one of them was an informant to Phineas Shattuck he could not doubt, given Adcock's story and the fact that the heel flies had known where the Hubbard women were going. He had no reason to doubt that the informant had shot Vance Hubbard in the back. He suspected from the grim purpose in Tyson's face that this was gnawing relentlessly at the young man's innards.

If Owen had spent long enough in the camp to become better acquainted, he might have an idea who now was about to betray the men in the thicket to Shattuck and the soldiers.

Tyson slapped the palm of his hand soundly against the horn of his saddle. "Red Upjohn!"

"Hunh?"

"Red Upjohn. He's the one. I know it."

Owen's mind raced as he tried to remember details. "What makes you think he's the informer?"

"I never liked him in the first place, always a troublemaker in camp, never satisfied, stirrin' up first one and then another to be dissatisfied. He never did really like Vance."

"I reckon he had reason to be that way, seein' a son lynched as a Unionist."

"He *said* his son was lynched. His word, was all. I don't remember anybody in camp ever sayin' they knew anything about it except what he told them. I don't remember anybody ever sayin' they even knew him before he come into the thicket. They taken him on his own say-so."

Owen thought back on the morning Upjohn's saber had punched him none too gently awake. He had had a feeling then that Upjohn would have killed him simply out of suspicion, had it not been for Banty Tillotson's intervention and Mary Hubbard's pleading. Later he had accepted the explanation that Upjohn was bitter against all soldiers because of what had happened to his son. He remembered other allowances he had made.

Owen said, "I'm tryin' to remember just where he was ridin' the night you-all took us out of that jail, the time your brother was shot."

Tyson replied crisply, "You had to be held in the saddle, so you wasn't seein' anything very clear. But *I* can remember. Upjohn was somewhere behind us."

"So were a bunch of others, I expect."

"But I remember Upjohn hangin' back, shootin' at the ones that was shootin' at us . . . so he said. And when Mama told your daddy about Uncle Ed and Aunt Vi, Red Upjohn was standin' there listenin'."

"It wasn't exactly a secret in the camp."

"It was him," Tyson declared. "It was him. And he'll lead Phineas Shattuck and the soldiers into the thicket . . . if I don't kill him first."

They were within a short distance of the thicket when they rode over a hill and came suddenly upon a troop of soldiers taking their rest, cooking their supper. Pulse racing, Owen looked for a way to run, but there was none. They would be overtaken or shot before they traveled a quarter of a mile.

Tyson reached for the pistol in his belt. Owen grabbed his arm. "Don't be gettin' us killed. Keep your mouth shut and let me do the talkin'."

A tall man wearing a gray coat, the only remnant of a once-proud uniform, stepped out into the trail and raised his hand. "You men hold up there. Identify yourselves and state your business on this road."

A bar on his shoulder identified him as a lieutenant. He was backed by enough soldiers to make any order nonnegotiable. Swallowing his doubts, Owen saluted and once again tried to be a good liar. "We're from B

Company, sir. They're up ahead of us, on their way to join a home guard outfit and somebody named Shadrack."

"Shattuck," the lieutenant corrected him. "How is it that you have fallen behind the rest of your unit?"

"Our horses went lame, and we had to recruit a couple of replacements. Captain said if we didn't catch up by dark, he'd nail our hides to the fence." It seemed a plausible enough story. Owen modeled it after an experience six months ago back east.

This lieutenant believed it or said he did. "It will be dark shortly, and you are not about to catch up that soon. You men will join my company for the night. We are all traveling the same direction."

Owen argued, "The captain is real particular."

"I'll explain to him when we catch up to your company. I feel he would not want you men to become lost and find yourselves in some tavern instead of your appointed place." His firm manner indicated he expected unconditional obedience. Any further argument might arouse his suspicion.

Owen glanced at Tyson, trying to tell him with his eyes that this was no time for doing something foolish. "We're obliged to you, sir. Just as long as you'll make sure our captain understands . . ."

The lieutenant accepted easy victory with grace. "You men attach yourselves to a likely mess. At least you shall not miss your supper."

A familiar voice spoke. "I know these men, Lieutenant. I'd be pleased to have them join me."

Owen's heart sagged as a man stood up from his seat on a rolled blanket beside a campfire. He wore a black eye patch and had a streak of white in a dark beard.

Sheriff Claude Chancellor!

Chapter 9

Shaky himself, Owen feared the sight of Chancellor might cause Tyson to run. Tyson glanced toward his horse and a stand of scrub timber three hundred yards away, evidently weighing his chances.

Chancellor said in an easy manner, "I don't have much in the way of fixings, but I'd be proud to share with you boys."

Owen swallowed. "We'd be obliged." He wondered why Chancellor did not draw the revolver from his belt and place them under arrest. But when the sheriff moved his hand it was a friendly gesture, reaching out. Owen accepted with wariness. Tyson spoke not a word. He hesitantly took Chancellor's hand, though his eyes said break and run.

The lieutenant asked, "You'll vouch for these men, Sheriff?"

Chancellor nodded. "Their fathers have been friends of mine."

Dismay turned gradually to puzzlement for Owen, but he asked no foolish questions.

Chancellor looked at Owen's arm. "It appears that wound of yours has about healed."

Owen moved the arm for demonstration. "It's come a ways."

Chancellor told the lieutenant, "The Yankees gave him a remembrance, just as they did me."

That seemed to settle any lingering doubts the lieutenant might have had. "At least you men have been granted a chance to face the enemy and test your mettle. I have been relegated to this backwater to chase after deserters and ragtag Union sympathizers skulking in the thickets. Hardly the proper opportunity for a man to discover what stuff he's truly made of."

Chancellor's voice grated with irony. "The deserving are often overlooked, while others are blessed by opportunity."

The lieutenant missed the bitterness. "Spoken truly. Now I leave you gentlemen to your supper and attend my own." He walked across the camp to a fire where a black servant knelt stirring a pot. At least, Owen thought, the lieutenant was suffering in comfort.

Chancellor turned to his own fire, giving attention to a blackened tin bucket, its contents simmering on a small bed of red coals. "Beef stew," he said. "The remnant of a dinner which a kind old lady fed me at noon. She insisted I bring along what was left so I would not languish at nightfall."

Owen looked around apprehensively. "How come you didn't tell that officer who we are?"

Chancellor gave both young men a long, silent study.

"I am not Phineas Shattuck. I remember you boys from better days. And I remember your fathers." He gave Tyson his quiet sympathy. "I heard what happened to Vance. I've heard also that Andrew Danforth took his place in the thicket."

Tyson said sternly, "Nobody taken Vance's place." He glanced at Owen with defiance. "Somebody had to hold things together, is all."

Owen said nothing.

Chancellor declared, "I'm surprised to find you-all traveling openly on this road. It's foolhardy, to say the least."

Owen replied, "We found out there's been a spy in camp. He's fixin' to lead Shattuck and the troops into the thickets."

Chancellor nodded, a grim set to his jaw. "Did you find out who this spy is?"

Owen shook his head negatively, but Tyson said, "We know."

Chancellor stared into the heating bucket of stew. "If you should confront him, I hope you'll remember that he regards himself as a man of duty, the same as yourselves."

Tyson demanded, "Was it his duty to kill Vance?"

"We do things in war that we would not consider at any other time. We kill our enemies."

Tyson's voice was edged with hatred. "Well, I know who *my* enemy is."

Chancellor said, "This war is like a dying horse, dragging to a pitiful end. We'll soon be able to put this insanity behind us and seek after friendship again. There'll be no need to call any man an enemy."

Owen nodded. "That's what my father said." It struck

him odd to hear the same thought expressed by a man who represented the opposite side.

Chancellor stirred the stew. "I tried to dissuade Shattuck from this big drive into the thickets. I told him there was no need, that to have the people holed up in the thickets is as effective as having them in jail. They can do no real harm there, and we don't even have to worry about feeding them. He said he wouldn't feed them; he'd *hang* them."

Owen grimaced. "He hates almighty hard."

Chancellor grunted. "For a purpose. He's taken your families' farms in the name of the Confederacy. If everybody who had any claim is dead, nobody can challenge Shattuck's rights. He'll buy those places from the government for a few cents on the dollar."

Owen blinked in surprise. That thought had never occurred to him. Tyson cursed softly.

An ironic smile came back to Chancellor's face. "You boys are young and innocent. You see patriotism in its pure sense. A man crafty enough can work patriotism for his own gain. The Confederacy means no more to Shattuck than it means to the lieutenant's pack mule."

Owen gritted his teeth. "Shattuck's a damned pig thief."

Chancellor shook his head. "He *used* to be a pig thief. He has advanced his family's name to major larceny." He shoved the long handle of a spoon beneath the bail to lift the bucket from the coals. "Sorry I have no bowls or cups. We'll have to pass the spoon between us."

Supper was lean and finished in little time. Chancellor nodded for Owen and Tyson to follow him. He strode to the army officer's campfire. "Lieutenant," he said, "since I have company now, I have decided to ride on to town before I sleep. I'll take the responsibility for these young men."

The lieutenant had no quarrel with that, and the three were quickly in the saddle. Owen looked back nervously, watching the several flickering campfires recede in the distance. He still puzzled over Chancellor's intentions.

Tyson Hubbard said suspiciously, "Chancellor, if you're figurin' on turnin' us over in town, you better think some more. We've still got our guns."

Chancellor gave him a look that bespoke a strained patience. "If I'd wanted your guns I would have taken them as soon as you entered that camp. Too many good men have died for no reason. I want you-all to go into the thicket and warn everybody to pull out while there's time. Scatter like quail. Let the pig thief find an empty sty."

Tyson's suspicions would not let him believe. "You ain't just lettin' us go."

"I am, as soon as we are safely beyond sight of camp. The invasion won't start until that company makes rendezvous with Shattuck and the others."

Owen asked, "Will you be with them when they come in?"

"It would be taken as strange if I did not go along. And how else would I be able to see the look on Shattuck's face when he finds himself holding an empty sack?"

Presently the trail came near to the heavy, brooding mass of the thicket, blacker even than the darkness that surrounded the three horsemen. Chancellor said, "This is a good place."

Owen extended his hand. Tyson did not. Owen said, "Mr. Chancellor, I won't forget what you've done for us."

"I hope you will, at least until this wretched war is over. It would not do for the wrong people to know. Godspeed."

Tyson spurred off in a lope toward the forbidding blackness of the timber. Owen did not call after him; the sound might carry back to the soldiers. He struggled to catch up because he would have difficulty finding Tyson once he entered that dense thicket. To his relief, Tyson reined in and waited for him, angrily admonishing him to hurry up.

Tyson said, "I don't trust that sheriff. I want to put as many miles between us and him as we can."

"Chancellor's an honest man."

"I don't trust any Confederate. And I'm rememberin' that you're one. If you want to ride with me, you'd better keep up." Tyson began picking a course through the tangle of brush in the poor light of a rising moon. Fortunately for the horses, he was forced to a walk, often a slow one. Keeping pace with Tyson presented no challenge to Owen now. He suspected Tyson had only a vague idea where they were, but after daylight his familiarity with the thicket would bring him to the dissident camp. For now, the main concerns were to travel in the right general direction and not break down the horses.

A couple of times during the night Tyson dismounted, loosening the cinch to let his mount rest. His voice, when he spoke at all, was curt. Owen harbored an uncomfortable feeling that sooner or later he and Tyson were due a confrontation, that would leave one of them— maybe both—bruised more than a little and leaking blood on the ground. He smiled grimly when Tyson rode headlong into a heavy, low-lying branch and cursed at the bite of the thorns.

Maybe that'll drain a little of the contrariness out of him, he wished. But anger and grief had eaten too long at Tyson. They would not be easily dispelled.

Daybreak found the two men in a small clearing, resting their horses and waiting for enough light that Tyson could determine where they were. One place in this thicket looked the same as another to Owen. He realized anew how helpless he would be here by himself. Difficult or not, Tyson Hubbard was a necessity. Tyson walked restlessly around the clearing, peering into the brush. At length he returned to his horse and tightened the cinch. He said nothing, but his manner indicated that Owen had better do the same or be left behind. Tyson set out toward the southeast.

Owen queried dubiously, "You know where you're goin'?"

Tyson replied crisply without looking back, "If you don't like my direction, there's aplenty of others."

Owen knew he must follow or soon be lost. He must trust to Tyson's familiarity with the thickets and, beyond that, to Providence.

At length Tyson reined up, looking around first with hope, then with certainty. The relief in his face revealed that he had secretly worried he might not find his way. "We ain't far off," he said. "I just hope your daddy ain't taken a fool notion to move camp."

Defensively Owen replied, "Anything he's done, I expect he's had a reason."

Tyson glanced back, surprised. "Kind of changed your tune about him, ain't you?"

"Don't get the wrong idea. I haven't changed sides."

They came upon the camp with a startling suddenness. A lean, ragged sentry stepped out in front of Tyson, rifle hanging at his side. He asked needlessly, "Hey, boy, you back?"

"You damn betcha," Tyson replied tightly. "Where's Andrew Danforth at?" He did not wait for the reply, which followed after him in an exasperated tone. "You'll find him over yonder at his tent, if he ain't somewhere else."

Andrew Danforth was sitting on the ground in the sunshine, oiling a rifle. He looked up quickly, then pushed to his feet with alarm. "You boys are supposed to be a long ways from here. Where's the womenfolks?"

Tyson said, "They're all right, but this camp ain't."

Andrew Danforth stared past Tyson at his son. Owen stiffly climbed down from the horse and clung for a moment to the saddle, the weariness heavy.

"Son," Andrew said, taking a couple of tentative steps toward him, "I sent you away from this place. I sent you back to your own outfit where you said you belonged."

"I still belong there," Owen replied. He moved toward his father but stopped short. "Somethin' come up."

Tyson put in bitterly, "There's a spy in camp. He killed my brother. Now he's fixin' to lead Phineas Shattuck and the soldiers into this thicket. They're figurin' to hang every man they can catch."

Danforth took a long breath. He looked first at Tyson, then at his son, wavering between doubt and belief. "How'd you-all come to find out?"

Tyson told it. The account spilled from him with anguish and anger, leaving him atremble.

Andrew Danforth accepted with evident reluctance. "And who is this spy? Did the kid tell you that?"

Tyson's eyes were narrowed as they restlessly searched the camp. "He didn't tell us, but we know. Where's Red Upjohn?"

Danforth looked quickly to Owen for corroboration. Owen shrugged. "Upjohn seems the most likely."

"The most likely? Then you don't know for sure . . ."

Tyson's fists were clenched. "Sure enough to suit me. Where's he at?"

"He's on lookout down below the thicket with Banty Tillotson and Jim Carew. They'll let us know when the soldiers come and where they are."

Owen declared, "With Upjohn for a guide, Shattuck'll comb this thicket. There won't be any safe place to hide. It's best everybody to leave it and scatter." *Like quail,* Chancellor had said. Tyson had not mentioned Chancellor's part in helping them. Owen considered telling, for his father would be pleased in light of their old friendship. But he looked at the anxious men quickly gathering around to listen. If anyone here were to be captured and forced to talk, word of Chancellor's act might reach Shattuck. That would be poor thanks for a great kindness.

Andrew did not need to repeat Tyson's story or to give any orders. He stared solemnly at the threadbare, hungry-looking men around him. He said simply, "There's no more sanctuary. Each man had best follow his own inclinations."

The mood was more of disappointment than of fear, or even of anger. One man said, "There's other thickets. I've got kin in the rough country way out on Bull Creek. They've stood off soldiers ever since the war started. I expect they'd be glad to take in anybody that wants to go with me."

Another said, "The soldiers can't be everywhere at once, even if Red Upjohn *does* help them. I'll just keep movin' in this thicket and take my chances." That was the decision of many, to scatter in twelve directions and offer the troops no concentrated target. A half-blind dog might stumble upon a covey, they reasoned. It took a hunter to smell out a lone quail.

In minutes the camp began breaking up. Andrew Danforth watched with sadness as the men packed their few belongings and saddled their horses. He told Owen, "I don't expect that every one of them can get away. The soldiers would have to have the worst kind of luck not to catch a few."

Owen asked, "What about you, Dad? You're not goin' to stay here and take a chance on bein' amongst them?"

Andrew frowned. "They've become my responsibility."

"Not after they split up. I came back to make sure Shattuck doesn't catch you."

Pride came into Andrew's tired eyes. "You were free and clear, son, and then you turned around and came back for *me*."

"We've had our arguments, but us bein' on two sides of this war don't stop you from bein' my father."

"Or stop you bein' my son." Andrew put his arms around Owen.

Owen swallowed. The barrier of old angers that had built between them seemed to fade like a morning mist. He felt toward his father now as he had not since he had been twelve or thirteen.

Andrew faced south. "There's three men down yonder, standin' watch. You-all say one is a spy. Maybe he is, and maybe he's not. But at least two of them aren't, and I've got to give them a chance."

Owen said, "We might run right into Shattuck's soldiers."

"Not *we*, just *me*. I don't aim to risk you boys."

Owen said, "I didn't come back to see you go off and leave me."

Tyson declared, "And I want to see Upjohn. Over my sights."

Andrew's voice went stern. "If he's with the soldiers, we'll know he's the one. If he's not . . ."

Tyson's eyes pinched with impatience. "We goin', or we just goin' to stand here and talk about it?"

Andrew said, "If you're goin' with me, you keep your hands away from that gun." He looked to Owen as if to ask his help in controlling Tyson. Owen could only shrug. There was but one way to control Tyson—to sit on him.

They rode southward, most of the time in single file. Andrew led. Owen watched his father's back, remembering other times, happier times, that he had followed . . . to the cattle, to the field, into the timber to hunt meat for the table. He had followed with pride in those days. That pride had returned, and he warmed himself in the glow of it.

Considering the density of the thicket, Owen wondered how his father expected to find the missing men. But Andrew seemed to know where he was going, and he held firmly to his direction despite the turns and switchbacks made necessary for negotiating a path through the brush.

Owen turned often to look at Tyson, who followed closely yet seemed strangely alone. Tyson's eyes held grimly to the horsemen ahead of him, but his mind was elsewhere.

In time they came to the edge of the thicket without having encountered anyone. Andrew's face betrayed his worry. He said, "They figured to scout beyond the edge, to get a little more of a lead when the soldiers come."

He looked to the east, then to the west. He arbitrarily reined his horse westward, just outside of the timber. There being no need to ride single file, Owen pulled up beside him. Tyson continued to hold himself apart, trailing. They rode in silence, Owen's tension building as he watched the rise and fall of the hills in the direction of town. Sooner or later, probably sooner, Phineas Shattuck would come riding over those hills with enough soldiers to invade Mexico.

Andrew pointed. "Yonder's somebody."

Owen blinked, and he saw one horseman. The rider evidently saw them at about the same time. He hauled up for a minute, studying them with suspicion, then spurred into a long trot toward them.

Tyson cursed in recognition. "Red Upjohn!" He drew the pistol from his waistband.

Andrew pulled over beside him and laid a big plowman's hand on the barrel. "Put that thing up, boy. We don't know for sure."

"*I* know."

"I said put it away!"

Tyson swore under his breath but gave to the compulsion in Andrew's stern gaze.

When Upjohn was sure of their identity he put his horse into an easy lope. He reined up, giving the two young men a moment of surprised attention. "I thought at first you-all might be Banty and Jim. You seen them?"

Andrew's manner was calm. "No. We've seen nobody except you."

Upjohn glanced back over his shoulder. "We split up. We was supposed to meet in the woods over back of the old Baxter farm, but neither one of them ever showed up." He pointed. "The soldiers are on their way, Andrew. They'll be showin' up over that hill yonder pretty soon now. I'm afraid they may've caught Banty and Jim."

Tyson seethed. "Or maybe somebody handed Banty and Jim over to them."

Upjohn's red-bearded jaw went slack. He was taken aback by Tyson's sudden show of hatred. "What're you talkin' about, boy?"

Tyson drew the pistol. "I'm talkin' about *you*, spyin' on us, tellin' Shattuck everything we done. I'm talkin' about you shootin' my brother in the back. If the soldiers are comin', it's because you've pointed the way."

Upjohn blinked, incredulous. He looked at Owen, then at Andrew. "I don't know what put a notion like that in the boy's mind, Andrew, but he's wrong. You know what happened to my son. I wouldn't help the people who done that to him."

Andrew said, "I know what you *said* happened to your son. Now that I think on it, I don't remember anybody ever sayin' he knew it to be true."

"But it *is* true," Upjohn insisted, color rising. "And I sure ain't never spied on the camp."

Andrew gave him a moment's hard study. He turned to Owen and Tyson. "Boys, I believe him."

Owen was not sure, and he said so.

Tyson was beyond reasoning. His knuckles tightened on the pistol. Owen pushed up in the stirrups and threw himself upon Tyson. The pistol fired, and Tyson's horse jumped. The two young men plunged to the ground. Tyson landed on his back, Owen on top of him. Breath gusted from Tyson, but he struggled to bring the pistol back into line. Owen managed a grip on Tyson's wrist and twisted his arm.

Andrew stepped down quickly and wrested the pistol

from Tyson's fingers. Tyson struggled and cursed beneath Owen's weight.

Andrew said, "Red, I'm givin' you the benefit of the doubt. But I can't guarantee how long we can keep this young hothead under control. You'd better go, and stay out of his sight."

Upjohn replied, "Andrew, I swear . . ." He stared down at Tyson. "Boy, I never done none of them things you said. As for your brother, I disagreed with him some, but I never knowed a better man." He looked back at Andrew. "Except maybe this one."

Owen said, "You better go. I don't know how much longer I can hold him." Pain drove through his arm. He feared Tyson's struggling had undone some of the healing.

Upjohn pointed. "Somebody's comin' yonder, Andrew. You all better not stay in the open." Then he was gone, swallowed by the heavy brush.

Tyson cursed Owen and tried desperately to throw him off.

Andrew said, "Better let him up. There *is* somebody comin'." He squinted. "It's Banty Tillotson."

Owen turned Tyson loose and stepped to his feet. He tried to look at the incoming rider, but Tyson staggered him with a hard fist. Owen threw up his arm in defense, blinking, trying to dispel the blinding flashes that whirled before his eyes.

Andrew threw his arms around Tyson and pushed him back. "Stop it! The fight's over."

Banty Tillotson drew rein, studying the angry scene with amazement, then amusement. He broke into his familiar grin that Owen had found to be like morning sunshine in the somber camp. "You're the last people I expected to find here. I don't suppose you've seen Red Upjohn?"

Andrew nodded. "We've seen him. That's what this ruckus is all about. Tyson's got it in his head that Red's a spy."

Tyson spat. "And I'd've shot him, but they stopped me."

Banty asked, "Where'd you get a notion like that?"

Andrew put in urgently, "There's no time to be talkin' about it now. The soldiers are comin'. Where's Jim Carew?"

Banty replied, "There's no need to be lookin' for Jim. The soldiers have already got him." His hand went down to his hip, and it came up full of pistol. "They'll be here directly, and then they'll have *you*."

Andrew's mouth dropped open. "Banty . . ."

Banty said, "You-all just stay on the ground, where I can watch you. It won't be but a few minutes."

Andrew expelled a long breath. "It wasn't Red who was the spy in camp. It was *you*."

Banty nodded. "I never taken no pride in it, but they said it was my duty, and I done it."

Tyson choked for breath. "Did you . . . did you really shoot my brother in the back?"

Banty said regretfully, "He was a good feller, but he was my enemy. I seen a chance to put him out of the way with everybody figurin' some heel fly done it. I'm sorry, boy, but that's the fortunes of war."

Andrew seemed more sad than angry. "And now you're fixin' to turn us over to Phineas Shattuck."

"I never liked him much, but he's on *our* side."

Owen's gaze was drawn to movement at the top of a low hill. He saw what he took to be perhaps a hundred horsemen. His stomach knotted. They were his soldiers, his side. But they would hang him as if he had been a Unionist all along. In their eyes he was a traitor. The fighting he had done back east, the wound he had taken, would count for nothing now.

Andrew said, "My son is still a Confederate soldier. You know how he come to be caught up in all this. Let *him* go. Let both boys go."

Banty shook his head. "I wish I could. But I've got my duty. If it's any consolation, I'll be sorry about it."

Owen looked back toward the troops. They were coming at a steady pace, only a few hundred yards away.

Banty said, "If you've got anything you want to say to your Maker, you better be at it. Shattuck won't give you time."

"Did he give Jim Carew any time?"

Banty shook his head gravely. "None at all." He turned his horse half around to glance back at the on-coming soldiers.

The slap of a rifle shot startled Owen. Banty jerked in the saddle, then dropped to the ground, limp as an empty sack. His horse danced in fright, almost stepping on him. Andrew strode quickly forward and picked up the pistol where it lay near Banty's twitching fingers. Owen's mouth was dry as powder. He licked at his lips, but his tongue was dry too.

Red Upjohn rode out of the brush, black smoke curling from a rifle in his hand. "Them soldiers are almost on us. You-all better get mounted in a hurry."

Nobody had to be told twice. Owen gave the riders one glance as he swung into the saddle. He guessed them to be three hundred yards away.

Upjohn looked down on the fallen Banty. The eyes were open, but they showed no life. Upjohn said with a touch of regret, "I always liked ol' Banty. But I reckon he won't be leadin' them soldiers anyplace." He touched spurs to his horse. Owen and Andrew and Tyson followed him into the brush.

They rode hard, weaving, dodging limbs. Briars and thorns tore at Owen's clothing and gouged his flesh, but that was far preferable to what awaited if they did not outdistance Shattuck and the troops. They came in time to a stream that meandered through the thicket. They rode in it, finally moving out upon a mass of fallen, rotting leaves that would not betray sign of their passing.

When they felt safe enough to stop in a small clearing and rest the tired horses, Andrew said, "Thanks, Red. If it hadn't been for you and that rifle, we'd be dead now."

Upjohn shrugged. "If it hadn't been for your boy jumpin' on Tyson when he did, I'd've been dead before you."

Tyson's face flushed. He seemed silently mustering nerve to speak. At length he said, "Red, I don't know any way to tell you how sorry I am."

Upjohn gave him a long, angry study. "Boy, I don't even want to talk to you!"

Chapter 10

Owen was alone when he left the thicket in the pitch black that preceded the moon's rising. He followed the stars in a northeasterly direction, listening intently because he could see so little. It stood to reason that the soldiers would throw a picket line of sorts around the edge of the brush because their attempt at invasion had been crippled by Red Upjohn's rifle. The thicket was too immense for an adequate blockade by whatever soldiers the regional command could muster. Still, Owen could remember from his boyhood an awkward, stumbling pony that used to have a way of finding and falling into the only badger hole within a mile and a half. His own luck might be no better.

He rode all night without encountering anything more threatening than a few sleeping cattle. These moved aside but made little commotion that might attract attention of anyone standing watch in the darkness. Once the moon was up and Owen could see his way, he moved easier across country, skirting fields, hugging the timber where he found it, avoiding roads and trails where a patrol might wait. By daylight he judged he had put twenty or twenty-five miles behind him. He did not know how far Phineas Shattuck's authority and influence might extend. To maintain some edge of safety, he watered the bay horse in a creek just at daylight and rode into a grove of trees. The grove was within sight of a trail he had traveled with the Hubbards. He watched, but the only movement he saw was a couple of wagons, one laden with freight, the other with kids and chicken coops. Neither looked warlike.

He gave the bay several hours to rest and graze; he had been ridden long and hard the last few days. Owen felt no urgency beyond his wish to see Lucy again before he returned to that other war.

Toward noon a distant jingling brought his eyes open. A dozen horsemen moved down the trail in what he supposed was meant to be a military formation, though it was strung out and ragged, the men tired and listless. Owen's heartbeat quickened. He saddled the bay horse to be ready for a run should the soldiers make a move toward the grove. They had probably been part of the force that made the abortive push through the thicket and had come up empty-handed. Owen did not intend to give them cause for celebration.

They passed on down the wagon trail. Owen's pulse slowed, but he was nagged by a residual uneasiness. The bay could rest again when he had put more miles behind him. Owen gave the riders a while to be well beyond sight, then rode out the opposite side of the grove and around the hill, holding to his northeastward course.

Not until his second full day did he come upon another potential for trouble. It happened so suddenly that he had no choice but to play his hand for luck. Two horsemen rode from a motte of moss-strewn oaks. One raised a hand, signaling Owen to stop. The other balanced a rifle across his saddle.

Owen swallowed. To hesitate or to turn and run would almost certainly result in capture, or worse. At such a range the rifleman would have to be blind in one eye and nearsighted in the other to miss him. Owen hoped his face did not betray his anxiety. He forced a shallow smile, holding his right hand well away from the pistol in his waistband. "Howdy," he said.

The man who moved toward him wore a badge so small that Owen did not see it until it caught the sunlight for an instant. "You look like you're of an age to be a soldier."

"I am," Owen replied, trying hard but having to abandon the smile. He reached into his shirt pocket and brought out the leave paper given him at the camp hospital. It was becoming tattered along the edges. The lawman quickly scanned the page, frowning. "Owen Danforth, private. That you?"

"Yes sir."

"Says here you was given leave to recuperate from a wound. Where's it at?"

Owen raised his left arm. "It's still a little stiff, but I figure it'll be all right by the time I get back to the company."

The lawman still frowned. "Danforth. Seems to me I've heard that name lately." He glanced back at the other man, who only shrugged.

Owen swallowed again. It was probable that Shattuck had sent word about the Danforths beyond his own county borders. "We're a sizable family. There's aplenty of us around. None in jail, though, that I know of."

"Not everybody's in jail that ought to be," the lawman observed. He handed the paper back to Owen. "I've always been a man of faith, and I'll take it on faith that you're the man this paper talks about. You go on back to your company, soldier. You better hurry, though, if you want to get in on any more war. Talk is that it's about over with."

Owen did not have to feign surprise. "It's got that bad?"

The lawman nodded sadly. "We've run out of everything except cotton. The boys are about down to chunkin' rocks at them Yankees."

Owen's shoulders sagged as he remembered the ordeals he had endured, the friends he had seen die. He folded the paper and put it back into his pocket. Because it had bluffed him through the roadblock, it would probably pass him through others he might encounter as he moved even farther from home. To that extent, he felt relief. To the news about the war, he felt only regret over the sacrifices he had witnessed, terrible sacrifices now clearly wasted.

The lawman said, "Couldn't nobody blame you much, soldier, if you just laid up someplace and waited. I reckon you've already given your share."

"I'm still alive," Owen observed. "I've known a good many who aren't."

"Been too many paid too much. Don't get yourself killed on the last day of the war."

Owen came, in time, to the Bradshaw house where he and Tyson had been bringing Mary and Lucy Hubbard and where the waiting heel flies had changed their plans. He watched from the brushy knoll. He thought it likely the heel flies had given up and gone home before now. He saw a woman hoeing a garden and a man plowing a field of tall corn. He considered riding down to talk to them but regarded that as too much risk. The less these people knew, the better for them and for everybody else. He turned the bay horse away and left the Bradshaw place behind him.

Tyson had told him in a general way how to find the farm where Mary Hubbard's sister lived. Her husband's name was Josiah Wilbank, and it was said he raised some of the finest mules west of the Sabine River, or had until the Confederate army took them all for the war, paying him in scrip that would probably never be worth a secondhand chaw of tobacco. Owen found when he reached the vicinity that Tyson's directions had been too sketchy. He stopped at a farmhouse to inquire and found himself face-to-face with half a dozen young home guards who seemed of about the same caliber as Shattuck's. Their faces had known no introduction to a razor and needed none. But maturity was not a requirement for pulling a trigger, so Owen handled them with deference and showed them his document of leave. One of the youngest boys burned with curiosity about Owen's wound and pestered him to show it. An older boy had a greater sense of propriety and freely gave Owen directions to the Wilbank farm. "Anything to help out a soldier boy," he declared. "I'm goin' to be one myself, pretty soon."

Owen reflected on what the lawman had told him earlier about the poor state of Confederate arms but chose not to dampen the eager youngster's dreams of glory. "You'll make a good one."

He thought it high time the war was over and done with, before any of these boys became old enough to go.

The boy's directions took him to the Wilbank farm.

It was richer-looking than he had expected, the road
winding among great and ancient oak trees from whose
branches long beards of Spanish moss moved gently with
the wind. Nearing the large frame house, however, he
could see marks of poverty induced by the long war, the
old paint faded and peeled, the long wooden fences leaning one direction and another because there was more
work to be done than men to do it. As he had observed
in the heart of the old South, the larger the fortune, the
farther the fall.

He came upon the women gathering vegetables from
a garden just south of the big house—Lucy, Mary Hubbard, another woman he judged to be Mrs. Hubbard's
sister, and a girl of twelve or fourteen. The two Hubbard
women set down their baskets and hurried to the gate
to meet him. Lucy was first, eagerly throwing her arms
around him though half a dozen people watched. Her
mother hugged Owen, then stepped back with worry in
her eyes.

"Where's Tyson? And I thought your father might
come."

Owen explained the failure of Shattuck's invasion.
"They scattered out and tried to make a sweep, but they
didn't have Banty to guide them. It was easy to stay out
of their way, then cut back around them to where they'd
already been. Dad decided to stay and try to gather up
the men who didn't leave the thicket. Tyson stayed too.
Decided if he was to come here he might draw attention,
maybe get your folks in trouble."

Mary Hubbard frowned. "You sure they're safe?"

Owen told about seeing soldiers on the road. "Looks
to me like the troops've pulled out and left Shattuck no
better off than he was. Maybe worse, because the sol-

diers probably figure he put them to a lot of trouble with nothin' to show for it."

Mary Hubbard stared thoughtfully at Owen, then at Lucy. "You left Tyson in good health? And your father?"

"They're fine." He did not tell her about Tyson trying to kill Red Upjohn. She probably knew enough of her son's shortcomings without Owen adding to the list.

Lucy clung to Owen's hand. "And you? Would you stay here with us?"

He dreaded the look that would come into her eyes when he told her. "I'm goin' back to rejoin my company." Lucy's face was as sad as he had expected. He wanted to take her in his arms, but too many people were watching.

Mrs. Hubbard showed the couple a gentle smile. "Lucy, I would expect he's starved half to death. Why don't you take him in the kitchen and fix him some supper? We'll be in when we've finished here."

Lucy led him by the hand. When they were alone, behind the door, she turned to him with love, and wanting, and despair.

He stayed the night, for the Wilbank family assured him there was plenty of room. Their own sons had gone off to the war, their chairs vacant at the big table. One chair would remain forever unused. The young Wilbank girl stared into his face with shameless curiosity, giggling and turning away each time he looked at her. After breakfast Lucy followed him to the barn for one last embrace after he saddled the bay horse. The Wilbank girl was there, watching, paying no heed to her mother calling from the front gallery. Owen rode away, looking back until the great oaks hid Lucy from his sight. He continued northeastward, crossing the Sabine, setting out upon the muddy ground of western Louisiana.

He had been on the trail two weeks when he learned of Appomattox. He had quit dreading the soldiers. Occasionally, late in the day, he would come upon a detachment, show his leave document and spend the night in their camp, sharing whatever rations fortune might have vouchsafed them, and sometimes oats for the horse. Almost always, someone would try to trade him out of the big bay, arguing that if he was going into battle the animal would probably be killed anyway, and it was a shame to see such a one wasted.

One night he saw a campfire in the dusk and fell into the company of a dozen soldiers who looked as if they had just been sentenced to hard labor on the gun emplacements at Galveston. They were silent and morose, barely greeting him as he rode up. When he asked if he might join them, a hollow-eyed one who had not shaved in a month said with a shrug, "You'd just as well. Thirteen can't be no unluckier than this twelve. Whichaway you headed?"

Owen told them he was returning to his company. It would probably be somewhere back in Georgia, the best he could judge. The one who had spoken stared at him, his expression somber. "There ain't nothin' for you to be agoin' back yonder to. Ain't you heard? It's all over with."

"The war's over?"

The man nodded. "They didn't *whip* us. Ain't nobody can ever say that. They starved us out and run us out of anything to fight with. Lee's surrendered, but *I* ain't. I'm just goin' home. We're *all* agoin' home."

Owen clenched both fists. He was able to make almost as much fist with his left hand as with his right. "Two weeks I been tryin' to get back to my company. Now I find out I wasted all that."

"We've wasted a lot more than two weeks, friend. We've wasted four years. You'd just as well's to turn around. Whoever ordered you to go back, he ain't in authority no more."

Owen's gaze roved over the rest of the men. Their faces told him it was as the lawman had predicted to him, back in Texas. One of the men motioned for Owen to help himself to coffee. "We've brewed up the last we've got," he said bitterly. "Just as well drink your share and help us celebrate."

Owen accepted, for he had not tasted coffee since the Wilbank farm. He pondered what the men said and felt the infection of their dark mood. He turned to the bearded man. "You said somethin' about losin' authority. Who *has* authority now?"

"Nobody that had any kind of rank with the Confederacy. That's all gone. The Yankee soldiers'll be comin' along behind us . . . a few days, maybe a few weeks. *They'll* decide who's got authority. Won't be none of *us*, you can bet."

An idea brought a tingling to Owen. "What about home guards . . . people like that? They still have any say-so, you reckon?"

The bearded one shook his head. "They'll be lucky if the Yankees don't throw them all in jail."

Shattuck. Whatever legal authority he might have had was gone now, Owen realized.

The bearded one frowned at him. "You look like you're smilin'. What you got to smile about?"

Owen sipped the coffee and let the smile widen. "I was just thinkin' about a pig thief."

* * *

Strangely, as he started west again it seemed that almost everyone he met had heard the news before him. He wondered how he had missed it for so long. He stopped at first one place and then another, offering his work for a little food to see him on down the road. He found a dismaying number of hungry women and children who obviously had no food to give him, and he asked for none. Some of the women were bitter over the war and its failure. Others were only thankful that their men-folk—those who had survived—would be coming home.

At sunset, after crossing the Sabine into Texas, he came upon a little cabin badly in need of repair. Two small children watched bashfully from inside a sagging picket fence marred by broken and missing boards. Their faces were pinched and sallow. He knew by the look of them that food was scarce in this house, and he determined to pass it by.

A young woman stepped out onto the narrow little porch, shading her eyes against the glare of the fading sun. She watched him until it was clear he intended to ride on by. She hurried down off the porch and out to the gate, which hung by a single leather hinge. "Mister! Mister!"

He turned around, riding back to her and the two children. He took off his hat. "Yes, ma'am?"

She studied him with wide eyes. "You're a soldier, I'd take it by the look of you."

"I have been," he acknowledged.

"You seen anything of the Yankees? You know how long it's liable to be before they get here?" Fear was in her voice. It was not the first time he had heard the question, from men as well as women. It was usually asked with apprehension.

"No, ma'am, I got no idea."

She looked past him at the road, as if she expected to see the invaders just behind him. She asked quickly, "You got someplace you're ridin' to before dark?"

He admitted he was still several days from home.

The woman said, "Then you'll be needin' a place to sleep. There's room in the house."

There couldn't be much, he thought. Four or five paces would take a man from one side of the cabin to the other. And if there was any food in the place, it had to be miserably little by the looks of the woman and the two children who clung to her skirt. "I'd be puttin' you to too much bother," he said, looking for a graceful way to keep riding.

"It'd pleasure me . . . *us*. You go put your horse in the pen. If the Yankees was to come, I'd feel a lot better havin' a man around here."

"You got no man of your own?"

"He went off to the war. Ain't heard from him in over a year." Her tone carried a sense of desperation. "Please, mister."

He looked toward a small picket shed that served as a barn. "I wouldn't want to crowd you-all. I'll sleep out there."

He found a barrel in the shed but no oats in it. He led the bay horse out some distance and staked him in grass. Then he sought the woodpile and chopped wood until the young woman called him into the cabin for supper. It wasn't much, mostly greens she had gathered in the wild, and a little salt pork. He had looked in the smokehouse and found it empty.

A tallow candle burned on the table, making a valiant struggle against the gloom of the little cabin. She apologized for not having bread. "We run out of corn early in the spring. We'll be havin' some more pretty soon, out of the field. It's makin' good ears."

The children stared at Owen. He doubted that the smallest, a girl, could even remember her father. He did not want to voice his suspicion that the man of the house would never come home. The woman volunteered the possibility. "He wrote to us at first, and I reckon he wouldn't've quit writin' if he wasn't killed. My old daddy-in-law taken care of us awhile, but he died just after he done the spring plantin'. I don't know what's to become of us without a man on the place." He saw the wish in her eyes and looked away.

She said, "Ain't no tellin' what them Yankees might do, findin' us alone here thisaway." The fear came back into her voice.

He said, "They ain't goin' to hurt women and children."

"I don't know. I never seen no Yankees. But if they wasn't bad we wouldn't've been warrin' agin them, would we?"

At full dark she put the oldest child, a boy of three or so, into a crudely built bed softened by a cornshuck mattress. She rocked the little girl until she fell asleep, then placed her beside the boy. She tucked a cotton quilt around the children, then turned to Owen.

"This is a pretty good little farm. With a man on it, it'd make a fair livin'."

"I expect it would," he said uneasily, sensing where the conversation was leading.

"You ain't a married man, are you? No, I'll bet you ain't. You got a farm like this to go home to?"

He mumbled something that was not really an answer. She touched his hand. When he tried to pull it away, she held it. "You could stay here. You'd soon get to likin' this place. I'd see to it that you liked it." She drew closer, then was standing against him, body attremble. She said, "It ain't meant that people always be alone."

He wanted to pull away from her, and at the same time he did not want to. Her lips were parted, and he felt the warmth of her breath upon his face. A powerful temptation swept him, a hunger that demanded to take what was offered. He gripped her arms and felt the rising of blood in the woman as well as in himself. He sensed that she wanted him whether he stayed for the night or forever. But he sensed also that she might have wanted almost any man who happened upon this place at this time of fear and loneliness and vulnerability. He looked at the sleeping children in the edge of the flickering candlelight and forced himself to draw away from her.

"I'll be goin' to the barn," he said, not really wanting to. He hurried outside, afraid if he lingered the heavy urgency of their wanting might change his mind.

Were it not for Lucy, he might have stayed.

He heard the woman crying softly as he walked briskly away from the porch. He slept little, half expecting her to come out to him in the night, and wondering what he would do. He might not send her away.

He was up before daylight, saddling the bay. He remembered seeing a couple of deer dart from the edge of a field to the nearby timber as he had approached the evening before. He rode back the way he had come, working into the woods and riding slowly, looking toward the open ground beyond the trees. Soon he saw two does browsing amid scrub brush in the last short while before the sun's rising. They would take a bite, then look quickly around, ready to race the little distance back into timber at any sign of danger. Owen wished for a rifle but had only the pistol. He tied the bay horse and advanced slowly toward the deer. He used the trees for cover, moving only when the deer browsed, freezing his movement each time one jerked its head up. One seemed to look directly at him, and he feared it had spotted him. But it would turn its head away to nibble at a bush, and he would move forward a step or two. When he was as near as he thought he would be able to go, he braced the pistol against a tree. He aimed for a point behind the shoulder and fired. The doe jumped straight up, fell, kicked for a minute and went still. The other bolted.

He gutted the doe where she lay. As he was finishing he watched a rider on a black horse moving toward him in the pale light of sunrise. The stranger hailed him at some distance to assure him he presented no threat. As he neared, Owen could tell he was a young man, wearing the tattered vestiges of a once-gray uniform.

The horseman halted, smiling. "You goin' to need any help eatin' that venison?"

"Maybe," Owen replied. "Where you headed?"

The young man shrugged. "Damned if I know. Somewhere west. Ain't no use goin' back to Georgia. Yankees burned everything, from what I hear."

Owen smiled. "You hungry?"

"Last thing I ate was a slow-movin' rabbit, the day before yesterday."

Owen said, "There's a cabin down the road yonder, just around that timber. I was fixin' to take this deer meat to the lady who lives there, but I'll let you take it for me. I'll bet she'll fix you a good breakfast with it."

"You ain't comin'?"

"I got business on down the road. You'll save me some time if you'll deliver her this."

"I'll consider it a privilege."

Watching the soldier ride away, the doe tied behind his saddle, Owen thought of the woman and remembered the hungers which had ached in him last night. He could not truthfully have said that he turned away without regret. But he did turn away.

He came to the Wilbank farm late the following day, his heartbeat picking up at the anticipation of seeing Lucy. The fires kindled by the other woman had not quite burned out. Josiah Wilbank, working in the field, unhitched an old workhorse and rode out bareback to meet Owen on the road. "Been lookin' for you to show up," he said jovially.

"Lucy at the house?" Owen asked without taking time first for conventional niceties, beyond a hasty handshake.

Wilbank shook his head. "She and her mama left here three days ago, soon after we heard the war was over. They was anxious to get back to their own place."

"Their place was taken away from them," Owen worried, "same as ours was."

"But it was taken away under the powers of war. I expect the courts'll give it back to them easy enough, if it even has to go that far."

Disappointed, Owen said, "I figured we'd all go home together. I'd even figured maybe . . ." He broke off. He had entertained some notion of having the Wilbanks' minister marry him and Lucy before they started back. He saw no gain in telling Wilbank. No use telling anybody until he first asked Lucy. "I'd best be ridin' on, then."

Wilbank would not hear of that. He prevailed on Owen to spend the night, his young daughter plying Owen with all manner of personal questions from supper until bedtime. At daylight Owen was on his way.

He purposely avoided the town, for he had no way of knowing the political situation there, the dangerous resentments that might still be lingering from a war fought and lost, the opportunities for getting himself embroiled in some painful unpleasantness before he even got home. He skirted the great thicket and rode to the Hubbard farm.

To his surprise he found it deserted. He found no tangible sign that Lucy and her mother had even been there. It was plain enough that the place had been worked. The fields were cultivated, the corn plowed out. Phineas Shattuck had probably been responsible for that, expecting the fruits of the harvest for himself. He was going to feel mightily let down that the Confederate army had not adequately protected the spoils he had considered his own.

The hell with him, Owen thought. The Hubbards could well use whatever crops those fields would provide. He could see poetic justice in Shattuck's having done the work on stolen property, or having paid someone to, then losing it all.

Owen was vaguely troubled over not finding the Hubbards, for they had had time enough to have arrived here well ahead. But his disappointment about not seeing Lucy was soon lost in the excitement he felt over riding freely and without fear across land he had known since boyhood, land he considered home. He avoided the thicket, for he had never spent a comfortable moment in it. He had felt somehow choked by the closeness of the heavy growth. He had felt stifled, cut off from fresh air, from the open sunshine.

He came, finally, to the hill that overlooked the homeplace. He paused, looking down upon it, enjoying the sight of the green fields, the open pastureland where the Danforth cattle quietly grazed. He saw a thin gray wisp of smoke rising from the chimney, and his heart felt warm. He touched spurs to the bay's ribs. "You're fixin' to finally get some feed and rest, boy. You're home."

From a motte of trees a rider moved out to intercept him. A momentary flair of apprehension gave way as he remembered that the fighting was over; there was no reason any longer for fear.

Red Upjohn quickly disabused him of that notion. His horse was in a long trot as he rode toward Owen, his hand raised for a halt. Upjohn looked cautiously down the hill toward the house. "Come on, boy," he said urgently. "Maybe you ain't been seen."

"What's the matter?" Owen demanded. "The war's over."

"Everywhere else but here, maybe," Upjohn said, blocking Owen's path, motioning him back up the hill. "Phineas Shattuck ain't fired his last shot."

Chapter 11

Reluctantly, looking back over his shoulder toward the cabin that was home, Owen followed Red Upjohn in a retreat to the other side of the hill. Upjohn said urgently, "You've got younger eyes. Anybody comin' after us?"

Owen saw no activity around the house. "Who's down there?" he demanded.

"Some of Shattuck's crowd. They're layin' for you to come back, like they laid for your daddy and the Hubbards. Shattuck's got all them folks in jail."

Owen's eyes widened. "My dad?"

Upjohn nodded gravely. "Along with Mrs. Hubbard and her daughter. And that hotheaded Tyson. Charged them all with sedition."

Owen protested in disbelief, "But the Confederacy is dead. He's got no authority."

"He's got the guns. *That's* authority. He's still got a few home guard kids with him. Recruited some toughs

that don't mind grindin' their bootheels on other people's necks. Promised them a share, more'n likely, if
they'll help him hold onto what he's taken."

"When the Union soldiers get here, they'll set things
straight."

"Not if everybody who might contest him is dead."

Owen swallowed. "Dead?"

"Dead. He confiscated the Hubbards' land, and your
uncle's, and your daddy's. Then he bought it all from
the Confederate government for the price of a few good
saddle horses. Unless you Danforths or the Hubbards
take him to federal court, he'll keep what he stole.
You're the only one still runnin' loose. That's why he's
got to get ahold of you. Then he's got to see all of you
dead before the federals come."

Owen shivered. "You're talkin' about murder. They'd
hang him higher'n the Union flag."

"Not if there was some big, terrible accident nobody
could blame him for. I'm guessin' he has all that figured
out."

Panic threatened to overpower Owen. "I've got to
bust them out of there . . ." He reined the bay horse half
around.

Upjohn leaned down, cursing, and grabbed the reins.
"Hold on, boy, and think a little. Don't make it easy for
him. You're all that's kept them other people alive."

Owen's chill came back. Anger followed it. "What's
Claude Chancellor done about this? He's the *real* law
around here."

Upjohn's eyes pinched. "Way I heard it, he tried to
stop Shattuck from throwin' your daddy in jail, and
Shattuck bent a gun barrel over his head. Charged *him*
with sedition too."

"There's got to be some good people who wouldn't

stand by and let a pig thief get away with such as this."

Upjohn shrugged. "They're figurin' like you did, that the soldiers'll set everything right. But they ain't seen Shattuck from our side of the fence. They don't realize what he's capable of."

Upjohn pointed his red-bearded chin toward a thicket, then reined his horse into it. Owen followed, a dozen wild ideas racing through his mind. Most were akin to suicide.

Upjohn said critically, "That horse of yours looks like he's run out his string. You oughtn't to ride him so hard."

Damn it, Owen thought, *this is no time to be talking about horses.* But Upjohn was right. Without a good horse, he could do little to help anybody. He pictured Lucy in that miserable jail and clenched his fists. "I'll break them out of that place!"

"Sure you will," said Upjohn, "but not by ridin' in there like a big dumb calf to the slaughter. We got to think." He stepped down from the saddle and loosened the cinch so his horse could breathe easier.

Owen's hands trembled as he followed the example. "You said *accident.* What kind of an accident could kill everybody without Shattuck standin' the blame?"

Upjohn grunted. "Your daddy told me what happened to his barn after he tried to get Shattuck jailed for stealin' pigs. And I seen for myself what happened to your uncle's cabin."

"Fire!" Owen exploded. That *would* be Shattuck's way.

Upjohn gave him a moment to let the terrible picture take its full shattering effect. "As I recollect that old jail, it's built of lumber, dry as powder. Stands up high on wood posts. Wouldnt take nothin', hardly, to touch it off. It'd go up in a minute, with all them folks locked in their cells. There couldn't nobody prove Shattuck done it himself."

Owen shuddered in cold dread. The grisly logic was inescapable. It was just the kind of plan to take root in a mind like Phineas Shattuck's. It occurred to Owen that Red Upjohn also had such a mind, warped by bitter experience. Perhaps it took a man like Upjohn to understand a man like Shattuck and anticipate what he might do.

Upjohn said, "We'll rest these horses till dark. Then we'll slip into town and figure out what to do."

A stranger riding across country in the night could easily have passed the settlement without noticing it. Lamps cast a dull light through a scattering of windows, and lanterns glowed dimly on a porch here and there. Otherwise, the town was dark and devoid of welcome. Owen and Upjohn sat on their horses at the outer edge, watching and listening to the oppressive silence. A horse nickered, a baby cried. A dog barked somewhere, and a couple of others briefly relayed the message. Owen heard no music, no laughter. Life had turned Spartan and bleak here as the war had dragged on. Few people had either the money or the disposition to indulge themselves. Now he sensed that the psychology of defeat had laid a cold hand upon the place. Like other towns he had passed on his way home, this one waited in silent dread for the federal soldiers and an unknown future.

"Ain't much town," Upjohn observed. He had never lived here.

Owen shrugged. It was small and backward, judged against cities he had seen during his soldiering. Growing up miles out in the country, a rough-handed and unread farm boy, he had always suspected the townspeople looked down on him. He had been uncomfortable here. But never before had he felt like an enemy, infiltrating hostile lines.

He pointed for Upjohn's benefit. "That yonder's the livery stable and wagonyard. I heard Shattuck confiscated it when Dad Wilson tried to run off to Mexico. They caught up with the old man and shot him."

Upjohn grunted. "Convenient for Shattuck. I don't reckon Wilson left any relatives to take up his fight?"

"No." Owen knew what was on Upjohn's mind. His stomach felt cold.

Upjohn pointed with his chin. "Let's ease down yonder on the dark side of the street and take a look at the jail."

Owen rode as near the buildings as possible, noting the alleys for a possible quick escape. He stopped opposite the jail. From the open front door, a lamp cast a dim orange light upon the sagging wooden walk. A movement caught Owen's eye. A man stood in the doorway, blocking the light. He was no more than a silhouette, but Owen recognized the slouch. His breath came short.

Upjohn brought up his rifle. "This'll be easier than I thought."

Owen laid a shaking hand on the barrel's cold steel. "No. I won't do it thisaway."

Upjohn reconsidered. "You're right. You've got to live here; I don't. Tell you what to do: you ride on down yonder and go into that dramshop so people will see you. Then, when I shoot him, nobody can say you done it."

"You don't understand. I can't shoot him from ambush or have you do it either. I saw enough of that in the war. Maybe we can bust in and surprise him."

Two more figures came to stand in the doorway. Upjohn said, "We'll play hell surprisin' *three* of them."

"We'll figure somethin'. Let's move away from here before their eyes get accustomed to the dark." Owen pushed the bay into a narrow space between two buildings, half afraid Upjohn might fire the rifle anyway. But Upjohn followed him.

Presently they were at the back side of the corrals, behind the livery barn. A dozen or so horses stood in the pen, most at rest, a few tugging at hay piled in crude racks built of branches tied together. At the corner of the corral a hay shed sagged with age. Owen remembered that Dad Wilson used to keep extra saddles there for protection from the weather.

He said, "When we get the folks out of that jail, our best bet is to run for the thicket and wait there till the soldiers come. We'll need horses for everybody."

"*When* we get them out?" Upjohn shook his head. "You mean *if* we get them out. Best let me do it my way. Kill Shattuck and that'll be the end of it."

"Been too much killin' already."

The corral was not guarded; Shattuck evidently had seen no reason it should be. Owen and Upjohn quietly caught and saddled four horses. When Owen caught a fifth, Upjohn said, "We've got all we need."

"Claude Chancellor's in there too," Owen told him.

Upjohn grumbled that jail was the proper place for a Confederate sheriff. Owen told him of Chancellor's part in sending a warning to the people in the thicket. Upjohn reluctantly acknowledged that he might have redeeming qualities, even if he *was* a Confederate.

"*I'm* a Confederate," Owen reminded him.

"But you got a good daddy."

When the five horses were saddled, Owen opened the

gate and eased the others out into the town section, careful not to stir them to more than a gentle walk lest the sound of their running draw attention. He looked back at the hay shed. "When we wanted to surprise the Yankees we used to pull a diversion and draw their attention away from what we were fixin' to do."

"Shootin' Shattuck would be diversion enough. It would surprise the hell out of *him*."

Owen knelt and pulled some dry straw together. He took a flint and a steel from his pocket and struck sparks until one finally ignited the straw. When the blaze was large enough that the breeze would not blow it out, he kicked the burning straw into a pile of hay.

"Shattuck won't stay at the jail when he sees a fire at his livery barn. Let's move up yonder and be ready."

The blaze was quickly climbing into the shed as Owen and Upjohn led the saddled horses away. Upjohn grunted in dark satisfaction, looking back. "Shattuck'll squeal like a pig caught under a gate."

They tied the horses to a rack in darkness between two buildings, then hurried afoot to a corner where they could watch the front of the jail. Already, a red glow was building behind the livery barn.

From somewhere in that direction a voice shouted, "Fire!"

A man stepped into the door of the jail. Owen heard him declare, "Phin, it looks like your stable's burnin'."

Shattuck rushed out the door, cursing. He wasted but a moment in looking. "Come on," he hollered, "or I'll lose the whole damned thing!"

He struck an awkward run down the street. Two men followed him. From all directions, Owen heard shouting as more people discovered the fire.

"Now!" he declared. "We got to be quick." He

sprinted toward the jail door, pistol in his hand.

Though he had seen Shattuck and two others leave, he stopped by the door to listen. Hearing nothing inside, he rushed in, Upjohn a step behind him. His gaze swept the lamp-lighted room for another guard. There was none. In his haste Shattuck had left no one to watch the jail.

"Dad? Lucy?" Owen called excitedly.

Lucy's voice responded from behind one of the iron-barred doors. "Owen?" He saw her in a cell with her mother.

He looked quickly for keys but saw none hanging on the wall. He began pulling drawers from the desk.

Lucy shouted, "The bottom one, on the right."

Keys jingling in his hand, Owen fumbled at the first lock and forced himself to slow down. He swung the door open. Lucy threw her arms around him. He almost crushed her.

Upjohn stood watch by the door, rifle in his hand. "You-all better put off the lovin' till a better time."

Mary Hubbard yanked the keys from Owen's hand and hurried to another steel door. Owen said, "Dad! Tyson! We got horses waitin'. We'll make a run for the thicket."

Mary Hubbard said soberly, "Your dad can't be ridin' anywhere. He's shot."

Owen's breath almost left him. He saw his father lying on a cot, making only a feeble move to get up. His chest was swathed in bandages splotched red. Claude Chancellor lay on another cot, his head wrapped. He made no move at all.

Lucy said, "Mr. Chancellor can't travel either. His head's broken. Doctor Levitt says it wouldn't take much to kill him."

"Won't take much if Shattuck comes back. We can't stay *here*."

Andrew Danforth reached up for Owen. Owen squeezed his hand, hard. Andrew said weakly, "You oughtn't to've come here, son. We'll be all right when the soldiers arrive."

"You won't be *alive* that long if we don't get you-all away from this jailhouse!"

Mary Hubbard knelt beside Andrew and pressed her lips gently to his forehead. "Let's leave it to Owen this time."

Owen asked her, "You know somebody in town who'll take them in and not tell Shattuck?"

"Doctor Levitt would. He's been here twice a day to see after Andrew and Mr. Chancellor. He's got no love for Shattuck, or fear either."

Tyson Hubbard and Red Upjohn stared silently at one another, old grudges still bubbling near the surface. Owen said, "Tyson, you and Red fetch Mr. Chancellor. I'll get my dad."

He blew out the lamp, plunging the jail's interior into darkness. Lucy and Mary Hubbard helped Owen bring Andrew Danforth to his feet and walk him haltingly to the door. Owen stopped a moment for a look outside. The blaze at the livery grew larger and redder, the flames leaping high enough that they reached over the barn. "Let's go," he said.

Upjohn and Tyson bore Chancellor between them, the man barely conscious enough to move his feet. They moved out of the jail and around the corner, every step strained and painful. Lucy cried, "Owen, we can't keep carryin' them this way."

"We can carry them to the horses and then hold them

in the saddle to Doc Levitt's. Keep comin', before somebody sees us."

Somebody already had. In the dancing red light from
the spreading stable fire he saw two men hurrying toward him. Heart tripping, Owen drew the pistol from
his waistband.

Claude Chancellor's deputy declared, "You won't
need that. We come to help you." He got an arm around
Chancellor. The other man motioned for the women to
let go of Andrew, and he brought his own broad shoulders to the task.

Owen said distrustfully, "You wouldn't tell Shattuck . . ."

The deputy spoke Shattuck's name like a curse and
spat. Owen knew the other man then, the teamster Jake
Tisdale, whom he had met on the road when he had
come home wounded from the war. Upjohn glanced
questioningly at Owen, but Owen could only shrug.
They had no choice except to trust Tisdale and the deputy.

Tisdale said, "This town's had a gutful of Shattuck.
We just been waitin' for the soldiers to come and pull
his teeth."

They struggled to lift Andrew and Chancellor onto
the horses. Owen mounted the big bay and put his arm
around his father to keep him from falling. Tyson and
Upjohn rode on either side of Chancellor, who seemed
not to grasp what was happening. The two volunteers
walked ahead of the horses. Tisdale raised his hand once
and motioned the riders into the shadows as people ran
toward the blaze.

They arrived in a few minutes at the back of the doctor's frame house. Levitt stood on his little front porch,
watching the hay shed flames. Wind-driven brands had

spread them to the main barn. Jake Tisdale hurriedly fetched Levitt to the rear of the house. The doctor, a bent-shouldered old gentleman with white hair and a goatee, recognized Chancellor and demanded, "What're you people trying to do, kill that man?"

Owen said, "No sir, tryin' to keep *Shattuck* from killin' him."

The doctor offered no further argument. "The back door," he said quickly, trotting to open and hold it.

Gently they placed Andrew and Chancellor on two beds. Mary Hubbard stayed close by Andrew, holding his hand while the doctor explored the wound to determine if movement had restarted the bleeding. Levitt said, "He'll be all right, I think," and turned his attention to the groaning Chancellor. "Lucy girl, you'd best pull those curtains so nobody can see from outside."

The fire at the barn was crackling, leaping wildly. A couple of dozen people had formed a bucket brigade in a vain attempt to save the structure. Now they abandoned that effort and shifted their attention to nearby buildings, trying to keep them from catching. Shattuck stood in the dirt street, yelling for them to come back and help him. His shouting was to no avail.

Standing just back from the front door to lessen the risk of being seen, Owen watched the barn collapse in a great explosion of flame, flinging sparks high into the air to fall again in a blistering shower. Any building within a hundred yards stood in some jeopardy of catching a firebrand. Men ran in all directions, seeing after their own, leaving Shattuck to watch helplessly as his buckled barn went into the final contortions of destruction.

Owen thought bitterly, *That's one piece of plunder that won't do you any more good.*

Tisdale and the deputy helped the doctor examine the sheriff. Owen heard Tisdale assuring Chancellor, "It's us, ol' Pete and ol' Jake. We'll stay right here and see that nobody hurts you."

Upjohn warned, "We got to do somethin' about them horses. Somebody'll see them."

Owen forced himself away from the pleasure of watching Shattuck stomp in wild frustration. "Right. When Shattuck finds the cells empty he'll probably figure we ran for the thicket. We'll want him to keep thinkin' that." Followed by Upjohn and Tyson, he hurried outside. He unsaddled his bay and threw his saddle into the doctor's small buggy shed. "I wish you-all would lead these horses out yonder a ways. Hide the saddles in the brush and turn the horses loose."

Upjohn cast a grudging glance at Tyson. He was still unable to put aside what young Hubbard had tried to do to him. "Come on, boy. I reckon you've got sense enough for a simple chore like this."

The horses were almost instantly swallowed up by darkness. Owen turned toward the house, then flattened himself against the fence. He saw the dark figure of a man hurrying down the alley, carrying a firebrand in each hand. The flickering light touched upon the face just long enough for Owen to recognize him.

Phineas Shattuck!

Shattuck looked furtively to one side and then the other but did not see Owen pressed into the shadows. He moved in a trot, his manner making it plain that he did not want to be seen.

A prickling ran up Owen's back as he realized Shattuck's intention. He followed, holding to the shadows so the dancing light of the stable fire would not betray him. He froze in place each time Shattuck stopped. At the jail, Shattuck looked back a final time, then thrust one firebrand beneath the floor. Almost instantly, flames began to spread among old dry tumbleweeds blown under the jail, trapped against the foundation posts since last winter. Shattuck hurried around the corner. Owen did not follow, but he knew Shattuck was firing the other side.

This was what he had expected of the man, but the reality struck him like a sledge. *You cold-blooded bastard! You think your prisoners are still in there!*

Shattuck trotted back, watching over his shoulder. Owen pressed himself against a building, but not quickly enough. Shattuck stopped dead in his tracks, drawing his pistol.

"Who are you?" he demanded. "Come out here where I can see you."

Owen drew his pistol, then stepped into the open. The fire licked its way up the jailhouse wall behind Shattuck. The man's features were in shadow, but Owen knew the light of the flames revealed his own face.

Shattuck exclaimed, "You!"

"Me, Shattuck. And I saw what you did."

"Who you goin' to tell? You'll be dead, like them people in that jail are fixin' to be." Triumph was in Shattuck's voice. In his excitement he seemed to take no notice of Owen's pistol.

"But they're *not* dead. We already taken them out."

Shattuck wavered. He tried to look back at the jail without taking his eyes from Owen. Owen could imagine the thought that must be racing through Shattuck's mind. If anybody *was* trapped in the jail, he would be hearing cries for help by now. The only sound was the crackling of the fire, rapidly sweeping the old frame structure.

Shattuck seemed to realize something else. "It was *you* set fire to my stables."

"Not *your* stables, Shattuck. You stole them, same as you figured to steal our land. Now you've got nothin'. Wait till the soldiers get here. And wait till this town finds out you fired your own jail to get rid of your prisoners."

Shattuck's weapon blazed. Owen stumbled as a slug seared a streak across his ribs and knocked some of the breath from him. He gripped the pistol with both hands and tried to hold it steady upon Shattuck. The darting flames half blinded him. He squeezed the trigger once, then again, and he kept squeezing until the hammer snapped on a spent cap.

Shattuck was gone, disappeared into the darkness. From somewhere Owen heard hoofbeats, a horse running. He heard men shouting, rushing toward the jail. Someone yelled, "There's people in there! We've got to get them out!"

Owen staggered to the front of the blazing jail, blocking the men rushing at the door. "No," he told them, "don't get yourselves killed for nothin'. Nobody's in there. We already got them out."

Somebody said a flying brand from the stable fire must have been carried on the wind all the way to the jail. Owen declared, "No, Shattuck set it afire. He wanted to get rid of the prisoners. I shot at him, but he got away."

A merchant ran up to report that Phineas Shattuck had just taken a horse out of a pen behind his store and had spurred away.

Some of the men called angrily for a posse to ride after him, but calmer heads counseled that pursuit in the darkness was futile. Owen realized that, as Jake Tisdale had said, the town had simply been tolerating the man, confident that he would be put in his place when the soldiers came.

He pressed his hand to his burning ribs and felt his fingers go sticky with blood. But the bullet had done no more than cut a shallow furrow.

Red Upjohn and Tyson Hubbard spurred into the street. Upjohn jumped to the ground, fighting to hold the reins as his horse reared and squealed its fear of the flames. Owen told what had happened. Upjohn swore, then looked off into the darkness. "Shattuck probably lit out for the thicket. Well, he forced other people to stay in it. It's only justice for *him* to have to hide there."

Lucy Hubbard came running up the street, calling anxiously for Owen. She threw herself against him and pressed her head against his chest. "I heard the shots, and I was afraid . . ."

His ribs burned fiercely, but he held her and said nothing that might make her turn him loose.

Upjohn stared into the darkness. "Come first light, I'm goin' to the thicket and hunt for him."

Tyson said, "I'll go with you."

Upjohn pondered, his doubts strong. "I'd rather have a broken leg. But I suppose you'd trail behind me anyway. Better to have you where I can watch you than behind me doin' God knows what."

Chapter 12

Impatient for the sight of home, Owen trotted the bay horse ahead of the wagon to the top of the hill. His eyes followed the curve of the trail through the curing grass to the double cabin. No one was there, so far as he could see. Jake Tisdale and several townsmen had ridden out yesterday to call upon the guards Phineas Shattuck had left and invite them to vacate the county of their own accord before a less courteous committee escorted them to the line.

He pulled the bay horse out of the trail and waited for a determined-looking Mary Hubbard to bring the wagon even with him. Lucy Hubbard was beside her mother on the spring seat. She said, "At least they didn't burn the place down."

Owen glanced again at the cabin, glad it had not followed Uncle Zach's into a pile of ashes. "Shattuck wasn't here to help them think of it." He looked in the bed of the wagon at his father, lying on several thicknesses of blankets. "You all right?"

His father declared, "I *will* be when you-all get me home."

They pulled up in front of the double cabin. Owen looped his reins over a wheel and leaned across the wagon's sideboards. He helped his father rise to a sitting position. "Slow now."

Andrew Danforth waved his son away. "I can make it to the ground all right. Nobody has got to carry me."

Mary Hubbard declared, "You'll do nothin' foolish, Andrew. We'll help you, and that's that."

Owen caught a smile in Lucy's eyes and could not restrain his own. Mary Hubbard would not be a silent wife to Andrew. Owen suspected that when he was able to rebuild the burned cabin on Uncle Zach's place, he would not find Lucy silent and subservient either.

He had not asked her yet, but she was waiting. Her eyes had told him that.

Andrew let Owen and Lucy help him down from the wagon, then shrugged them off. Mary Hubbard took his good arm and led him to the dog run.

Owen said, "I'll go put the horses away." He turned back toward the wagon and stopped short. A horseman emerged from heavy brush by the creek. A couple of grazing cows were startled by his sudden appearance and moved in a half circle to get around and behind him. Owen squinted but could not recognize him. The rider slumped over the horse's withers, his head bowed so that his hat hid his face.

"Company," Owen said warily to Lucy, motioning for her to retreat to the open space between the two sections of the cabin. "Might be a Shattuck man comin' back." He drew his pistol.

Lucy said, "It's not. It's Shattuck himself!"

Owen blinked, not certain. As the rider neared he knew Lucy was right. He swore under his breath and stepped back into the dog run, his hand nervous on the grip of the heavy pistol. Lucy hurried to the wagon, ignoring Owen's call for her to stay where she was. She grabbed a rifle they had brought from town. She turned, waiting for Shattuck. In her face was the same ungiving resolve Owen had seen at times in her mother.

He said, "If anybody has to shoot him, let me be the one. I've already got a war on my conscience."

"You may miss," Lucy declared. "But I won't."

Owen saw no belligerence in Shattuck. Approaching, the man remained slumped, barely raising his head. Owen saw blood, dried and stiff, almost black upon the shredded remnants of a shirt. Shattuck held one arm tightly against his chest, as if it might be paralyzed.

The horse stopped a few paces from Owen. Shattuck wheezed, "Help me, you-all. They're comin' after me."

Hatred burned like a slow fire in Owen's belly. "Why should *we* help you . . . you of all people?"

Shattuck tried to steady his gaze, and Owen realized with a start that the man could barely see. Shattuck's face was the color of clay . . . the gray of death.

Shattuck seemed confused, frightened. "You ain't the ones I left here. Who are you?"

"I'm Owen Danforth."

"Danforth? The soldier?" Shattuck lowered his head as if he were on the verge of giving up. "*You* done this to me, boy. It was you put these bullets in me. Now them other two, they want to finish what you commenced."

"What two? Who's after you?"

The voice quavered. "I don't know. Never seen them

close. But they've dogged me like bloodhounds."

Red Upjohn, Owen realized, and Tyson Hubbard. They had not come back to town since the night of the fire.

Shattuck asked plaintively, "You fixin' to shoot me again?"

Owen said bluntly, "I'm studyin' on it. You got it comin'."

Shattuck's voice rasped a weak effort at argument. "It was war. The war's over now."

"It was over before you tried to burn my dad and all them others to death."

"You wouldn't kill a helpless man, not in cold blood. I can't even hold my gun." Shattuck broke into a spasm of coughing and seemed about to slide from the saddle. The sound was painful. Owen tried not to feel sorry for him.

Andrew Danforth's voice came from the dog run. "Don't torment the man, son. He's dyin'. Help him down."

Owen looked back at his father leaning against the doorjamb. "After all he done to you?"

"He's finished. He won't hurt me anymore, or anybody else. You'd help a sick dog if he came to you like this."

"Or put him out of his misery." Bitterness roiled like tainted meat in Owen's soured stomach. But he placed the pistol in the wagon seat, out of harm's way, and took a position beside Shattuck's horse. "All right," he said grudgingly, "ease down. I'll help you."

Shattuck's remnant of strength left him as he brought his leg over the cantle. He tumbled. Owen grabbed him. The stench of the wounds struck him like a stinking wet blanket slapped across the face. Shattuck cried out in pain.

Andrew said, "Better put him in the wagon and get him to town. Maybe Doc Levitt can do somethin'."

Owen doubted that. He had seen too many in this condition. "He'd be dead before we could get him half-way there."

Andrew's voice was determined. "You'll wake up nights wishin' you'd tried."

Lucy laid down the rifle and came to Owen. "I'll help you."

Shattuck dragged his feet as the two young people supported his move toward the wagon.

A voice hailed them from the direction of the creek. Two horsemen spurred out of the timber. Red Upjohn was shouting, but distance and the wind muffled his words. Owen thought he knew the gist of them. He said urgently, "We'd better put him in that wagon quick. We're apt to have our hands full."

Shattuck groaned as they placed him upon the blankets which had been a pallet for Andrew Danforth. He was not too far gone to hear Upjohn's voice. He pleaded, "They're here. Don't let them have me . . . please!"

Lucy promised, "We won't."

Owen wanted to warn her not to make rash promises she might not be able to keep. He turned away from the groaning Phineas Shattuck to face the grim-eyed pair who rode up within spitting distance of the wagon. Both looked haggard, but they also looked like hunters who had treed a long-sought quarry.

Upjohn said, "It's a handy thing that you've got him in that wagon, boy. Me and Tyson, we'll just haul him down to the timber yonder and finish the job you started."

Owen forgot that he had had the same notion himself, not ten minutes earlier. "We're takin' him to town, to the doctor."

Upjohn snorted, "He won't need a doctor. Step aside if you ain't got the stomach for it. Me and Tyson, we'll do what's to be done." Upjohn moved his horse closer. His pistol was in his hand.

Owen remembered his own, lying on the wagon seat two paces away. It had as well have been two miles. "He's mine, Red, not yours. I shot him."

"Then do it yourself, and make a better job of it this time. But if you don't, I will!"

Owen placed himself between Upjohn and Shattuck. "No. My dad said it, and he's right: the war's over. It's time for the killin' to be over too."

Upjohn's eyes were almost shut, hiding whatever lay behind them. He leveled his pistol on Owen. "You're in my way, boy. I come to kill him. Don't make me kill you too . . ."

Owen swallowed. He wondered what everyone else was doing but could not take his gaze from Upjohn . . . from Upjohn, and from the awesome muzzle of that pistol. Owen raised his arms away from his sides, as if they would shield Shattuck from fire. "I'm not givin' him to you, Red."

He thought he saw Red's finger tighten on the trigger. He took half a breath and held it.

Tyson Hubbard had sat silently on his horse all this time. Now he said gravely, "Better pull back, Red. If my sister don't shoot you, my mother will."

Upjohn looked at the girl, giving Owen a chance to cut his eyes toward her too. Lucy had the rifle trained somewhere about the second button on Upjohn's shirt, and her eyes were like flint. Upjohn glanced then at the dog run, where Mary Hubbard stood beside Andrew Danforth. She held a pistol in both hands. Upjohn stared at her, clearly agonizing over his decision. Slowly then, and carefully, he shoved his pistol back into his belt and brought his hand clear enough to show he presented no further threat.

"Hubbards!" he declared with frustration. "If the boy don't kill me, the women will." He looked from Mary to Lucy and back again, perplexed. "I thought you'd all want what I come to do."

Mary Hubbard said, "You're welcome here, Red Upjohn, so long as you come in peace. But if you're set on violence, you'd best keep movin'."

Upjohn shook his head. "I never knew there was so damned many crazy people anywhere." He swung down from his horse and said to Owen, "Go on, then. Take him to hell, if that's your pleasure." He turned toward the dog run. "Mrs. Hubbard, would there be anything here to eat? Me and your boy ain't put nothin' down in three days."

Owen and Lucy moved together. He touched her arm and found her trembling a little. So was he. He stared at her, wondering. "Would you really have shot him for Phineas Shattuck?"

She shook her head. "Not for Shattuck, but I'd've shot him for *you*. The state he was in, I was afraid he might shoot you first. I wasn't about to let him."

Owen put his arm around her. He did not know how to tell her what he felt, and he did not try. He turned to the wagon. "We'd better hurry and get started."

Lucy climbed up the wheel and onto the spring seat. Owen leaned over the sideboard to rig a shade that would keep the sun from Shattuck's face. The eyes were open, but he knew with a sudden terrible certainty that they did not see and never would see again. Shattuck had probably already been dead when Owen had faced Red Upjohn and that pistol. A chill shuddered through him.

Owen closed the sightless eyes, and he pulled a blanket over the man's stilled face.

Quietly he said, "There's no hurry about anything now, Lucy. We've got all the time in the world."